Tincup in the
Storm Country

Tincup in the Storm Country

A Western Story

Lewis B. Patten

Five Star Western
Thorndike, Maine

Five Star Western
Published in conjunction with Golden West Literary
Agency

May 1996

First Edition

Five Star Standard Print Western Series.

The text of this edition is unabridged.

Set in 11 pt. News Plantin by Warren Doersam.

Printed in the United States on permanent paper.

Library of Congress Cataloging in Publication Data

Patten, Lewis B.
  Tincup in the storm country : a western story /
Lewis B. Patten. — 1st ed.
    p.   cm.
  ISBN 0-7862-0593-8 (hc)
  I. Title.
PS3566.A79T56   1996
813'.54—dc20

95-42549

Editor's Note

An earlier abbreviated version of this novel first appeared in *Giant Western* in October, 1953. Sometime later, after the author had set about to expand it for publication as a book, his agent could find no publisher who wanted to take it on due to many of the mature themes regarded at the time as far too controversial in a Western story. Now at last *Tincup in the Storm Country* can be published as its author had intended. The text is derived from Lewis B. Patten's own typescript.

Chapter One

Fall came to the high country. Night's frosty breath, blowing out of the north, stained the quakie leaves bright yellow, the sarvus orange, and the scrub-oak a rusty ochre. Grass underfoot, long and dry, rustled as the beef herd moved through it. The cattle turned at the urging of two riders who had galloped around to head them and then, still prodded from behind by the bulk of the crew, filed down the long draw towards the rim.

There were twelve hundred steers, mostly triple-wintered but with a few four-year-olds among them. Martin Joliffe experienced a feeling of solid satisfaction in watching them file past, for the whole year through this was what every hand on Tincup worked towards. This was the end of the beef roundup and the start of the drive to the railroad.

Tincup's foreman, Floyd Timmons, twitched the reins of his horse and rode past Mart. He said, "I'll take a swing down on the point and make sure there ain't no more shaded up in the spruces above the rim."

Mart shook his head. Abruptly the satisfaction of the moment was gone from his pale eyes, and there lurked instead in their depths plain shame and guilt that did not escape Floyd's notice.

"No," he said. "I'll go with you. I've stayed off that point all summer because I didn't want to remember what was down there at the bottom of it. A man has got to face things some time." He swung away and kicked his horse into a swift trot.

Floyd took off his dusty black hat and ran a reflective hand across his damp hair. Then he followed.

Mart did not look back. He was thinking how a man got to dreading some things, how, when he did, it was time to start facing them. There would be no help for Mart in letting Floyd ride the point alone. It was a thing he had to face himself.

All of Tincup's roundup worked towards this point, this finger of high land which marked the southernmost tip of Tincup's vast summer range. They gathered this ridge as they came, pushing the beef before them, dropping she-stuff, calves, and steers too young to ship behind. The trail sloped down through the rim a mile from the ridge's end, and this always left the long point for someone to ride at the very end of the drive.

Floyd's offer to ride it had been considerate, Mart realized, even though Timmons's thoughts cherished no blame for the thing that had happened here early in the spring.

Mart's own thoughts were the source of what blame was here. His own mind was where the seed of guilt kept growing.

The trail kept to the ridge's spine, almost to its exact center. If a man looked closely, he could still see evidences of the damage four thousand cloven hoofs had wrought in the grass roots as they crowded and pounded towards the four-hundred-foot drop at the end of the point. The point was like a funnel narrowing inexorably so that, when you reached its end, there was nothing left, nothing save the drop into empty space.

A vagrant twist of the wind, which at this time of the year came almost altogether from the north, lifted up the face of the rim, bringing still the sweet, nauseating odor of decaying flesh. Mart reined his reluctant horse close up against the edge of the drop and looked down, holding the fidgeting and frightened animal still with a ruthless hand. Floyd reined up beside him, also looking down.

Sheep made a grayish mass down there, but here and there a carcass picked clean by the vultures had bleached and now shone pure white in the afternoon sun. A gray cloud hovered over the mass, and Joliffe knew that this cloud was composed of flies. A buzzard, feeding, was but a speck at this distance. Mart's horse kicked over a rock and, after an interminable period, it hit the slide below and startled the vulture, startled, too, an old dog coyote who ran, a lean gray shadow on the sun-washed slide. Mart could hardly repress a shudder.

Floyd, still faced, said, "Boy, there's no damned use in blaming yourself for this. You've been brooding about it all summer, and you've got to quit it. Raoul gave the order to do it and, if you'll think about it, you'll have to admit it was the only thing he could do."

"I know, Floyd." He reined around, putting his back to the ghastly sight and rode along the rim, poking, with but half his mind alert, through the tall spruces that fringed the rim-top. Floyd watched him somberly from behind and at last wheeled his horse and headed along the rim on the opposite side of the point.

A steer got up in front of Mart and lumbered, crashing through the timber. Another joined the first. Mart had three ahead of him when he broke from the timber and rode down the draw towards the cattle that had bunched and now awaited their turn on the narrow trail. He let them go and halted, fishing a sack of tobacco from his vest pocket. He shaped a cigarette absently and touched a match to its end. Floyd came from the opposite side of the ridge with a single steer, pushing it into the bunch and then rode up beside Mart.

Floyd asked roughly, "What would have been a better way to handle Robineau?"

Mart shrugged. He shouldn't let Robineau's sheep bother him this way. He had told himself this a thousand times, but there was a vast gulf between telling and doing. Robineau had asked for what he got. This was Tincup grass, had been so since the Ute nation had surrendered it to the whites.

"It's free range, ain't it?" Robineau had asked defiantly.

"Free?" Mart had laughed without amusement. "Hold your sheep on it and you'll find out it ain't quite free. It's Tincup grass because Tincup claimed it when no one else wanted it, because Tincup has held it since, and because we'll keep on holding it."

It was some consolation to Mart to recall that he had not proceeded against Robineau at once. He had warned the man repeatedly and had only acted when Floyd Timmons brought him word that had the sheepmen in eastern Utah were only waiting — waiting to see if Robineau would make his grab stick.

Well, he hadn't made it stick. His sheep lay rotting at the foot of the rim. And the others had found their summer grass elsewhere. It might have been worse. Men might have been killed, but for the decisive way Mart had moved, throwing Tincup's entire crew against the sheepmen so that a fight would have been suicide.

Yet he couldn't forget the undulating mass of gray, woolly backs, crowding, pushing, bleating — moving like a tide to the end of the point — disappearing. He couldn't forget the mind sickness that obsessed him for a week afterward, that still obsessed him at times. He couldn't forget the way Robineau had looked — not angry, not even hating, just beaten . . . thoroughly beaten.

Floyd said sharply, "Marty! You got to forget it. If you had refused, Raoul would have made me do it. And if it hadn't been done, you know as well as I do that it would be sheep coming off the high country today instead of cattle."

"No. We'd still have brought cattle off."

Floyd's voice rose. "In what kind of shape? Skinny. Poor. You'd be shipping Tincup she-stuff too, because you'd know there wouldn't be feed for them next summer. Tincup would be through as a ranch, and you damned well know it!"

Mart shrugged. "I guess you're right." He made himself grin at Floyd.

The cattle made a long, red, serpentine column that crawled slowly down the trail. Shadows lengthened. Dust lifted from the cattle's hoofs, and the shouts of the crew raised in the still air, sharp and clear. Dusk came on, and the last of the steers lumbered off onto the trail. Mart and Floyd, and the rest of Tincup's crew, fell in behind.

John Robineau sat in his bare hotel room, three hundred miles to the eastward, and stared out the window at the same gray dusk. His sheep were gone, the fruit of a lifetime's work — all for one mistake, all because he had guessed he could make a steal of Tincup's grass stick, and because he had been wrong. He fondled the heavy Navy Colt revolver he held in his lap. Fondled it and lost his courage as he had lost it so many times before. He saw Lucille coming down the street, small and pretty and red-haired, coming back from work.

Perhaps it was the droop in her shoulders that gave him the courage he needed. Perhaps it was the sudden realization that he could never be more than he now was, an old man, a tired one, a beaten one. He could never be more than a drag on his daughter who must work twice as hard to feed two as she would to feed one. Before he could change his mind, before he could lose his courage, he thrust the muzzle of the Navy revolver into his mouth, thumbed back the hammer, and pulled the trigger.

Lucille heard the shot as she entered the shabby lobby. At once her weariness was gone, replaced by an intensification of the fear she had been feeling for weeks. With no real surprise, she saw him as she came into the room, slumped on the floor.

Now it was shock that she felt, and the empty, terrible sense

11

of loss. Later tonight, she would grieve, but before morning she would begin to hate — to hate the man, the ranch, the greed that was responsible for her father's death. Later the hate would turn to bitter gall and in the still, cold hours of dawn would begin her plan for revenge.

Chapter Two

On Thursday evening the herd arrived outside the town of Cedar City, slow moving, patiently plodding. There, Mart reined aside.

Floyd, stocky and graying, rode over beside him to say, "Go on, Mart," grinning with cheerful derision. "You can't keep a girl like Rose waiting. I'll see that the cattle get to the pens all right. I'll make the arrangements to load them in the morning. Go on."

"All right, Floyd." Mart Joliffe returned the foreman's grin.

Dust caked Mart's face, turning it a peculiar, grayish hue, hiding its healthy tan. His eyes were rimmed with mud where moisture from the eyes had mingled with dust. His teeth were white, big and solid like all the rest of him.

Tincup's beef roundup had taken six hard and grueling weeks. The strain of roundup, where Joliffe would drive no man harder than he drove himself, showed in the bone-weary sag of his wide shoulders, in the oddly inert way he sat his saddle. But anticipation danced now in his pale blue eyes, and his wide mouth stretched out and smiled.

To Mart Joliffe life was a series of tasks, each entirely separate from the others. When one was done, he put it behind him and promptly forgot it. Roundup, the year's most satisfying task, he now relegated to the past along with other things entirely finished and turned his glance towards the town, lying squat and ugly on the banks of the Little Snake River.

His horse broke into a trot as it entered the dusty length of Main Street, but Joliffe reined up short before Stoddard's

Saloon, still grinning a little, thinking, "Hell, she can wait until I wash the dust out of my throat."

He was tall, tall and solid — big boned. He banged open the saloon door and stood for a moment looking into the gloom, trying to accustom his eyes to this after the glare of autumn sunlight outside.

Pete Stoddard, behind the bar, said to someone patiently, "Go lead him over here to the bar. He's dazzled by all that gold on the hoof he's been driving ahead of him for the past six weeks."

Mart's grin widened. He walked, loosely relaxed, across the sawdust floor to the bar. He said, "I think I'll sleep a week." He looked at Pete for a minute, and finally finished, "Well, maybe I'll wait 'til tomorrow to start."

Stoddard chuckled.

Mart tipped the brown bottle and poured himself half a tumbler of its amber content. He downed the first one quickly, feeling the burn of the whiskey against his throat, raw from dust and shouting. Talk murmured through the saloon, working men's idle talk, talk about horses and weather, grass and hunting. Mart poured his second drink thoughtfully, letting the warmth of the first course through his body.

Pete Stoddard, tall, hollow-chested, and thin, put his elbows on the bar before Mart and said, "By golly, Mart, I'll sell more whiskey tonight than I have for six weeks. But I wonder if I ain't gettin' too old for that much excitement."

Mart grinned at him. "I'll buy until ten o'clock. I'll pay for the damage, too. Six weeks is a long time."

"They know you'll pay the damage. Maybe that's why there never is very much."

Mart tossed off his second.

Far up the canyon to eastward a locomotive wailed, and Stoddard automatically dragged his heavy silver watch from his pocket and looked at it to check the time.

Mart tossed a dollar on the bar and turned away. A warm glow was in him from the whiskey and a lift in his spirits, a lift that made him forget some of his aching tiredness. As he put his hand on the door handle, someone gave it a push from outside, and Mart stepped back instinctively. Odd this feeling — this feeling of almost physical revulsion.

Howie Frye stepped into the saloon and laid sour, mocking eyes upon him. Howie's thin, pale lips drew away from his yellowed teeth. He made a mock bow.

"The cattle king. The great man. The sheep-slayer."

Mart's great hands fisted, and Frye laughed softly, triumphantly. His face was seamed and sharp, his eyes as cold as the Little Snake in February.

Frye muttered: "Go ahead, Marty. Hit me. I'm half your size, so that ought to be about right. You can lick me easy, almost as easy as you licked Robineau."

The veins in Mart's forehead bulged. Trust this one to find his only sore spot and probe it constantly with his cruel, mocking barbs. Frye stood blocking the door, his spindly legs spraddled out, his thumbs hooked in his belt. Mart, fighting for control, tried to nudge past him, thus giving Frye fresh ammunition.

"The great man's in a hurry," he said, facing the bar and talking to Stoddard and to the others. Then he swung back to Mart, whining, "You don't have to shove us common folks out of your way, Marty. We'll move aside for you." He made a ceremony of stepping aside, then saying, "Going to see Rose, huh? In a hurry?" His voice rose, assuming a violence that was strangely akin to madness. "Damn you, Mart, some day, king or not, I'm going to kill you! You hear that? I'm going to kill you! But I want to see you in the gutter first. I want to see you broke . . . and hungry . . . and down in the dirt in front of your throne."

Mart spoke between clenched teeth. "Shut up, Frye. Shut up." His hands were fisted again, in spite of his efforts at control. He looked wildly at the sun-washed street, near yet so damned far. Because he couldn't run, and he couldn't fight. He had to stand and take Howie Frye's abuse.

"Go on! Go on! Rose is waiting for you . . . with open arms. She saw the herd at the edge of town from her hotel window."

Mart looked at Howie and was astonished to see that the man was shaking. He stepped past Frye and into the street. Wildness and violence flared in his eyes. His jaw was hard set, his teeth clenched.

If Howie had not been Rose's father, Mart would have said his trouble was jealousy. He could think of no injury Frye had suffered at the hands of either Mart Joliffe or Tincup. Could it be simple jealousy because of Tincup and the wealth that flowed from it? Or had Howie some secret grudge against Raoul? Mart shrugged.

He guessed that whoever had the wealth, the power, must always be subject to these violent hates in people like Howie Frye. Yet it never ceased to be a source of wonderment to him that a girl as sweet and beautiful as was Rose could be the offspring of a man like Howie who was bitter, vicious, sour, and vindictive.

The meeting with Howie Frye, a task completed, was harder for Mart to put behind him than most. Yet if he had learned nothing else from Raoul Joliffe, he had learned this — that worry over things that cannot be changed drove more men to their graves than any other single cause.

Frye was a recurring task, an unpleasantness every time he saw the man. And Frye had somehow divined the guilt that tortured Mart over the Robineau sheep. Recalling that again now, Mart thought, *Floyd is right. What else could I have done? Killed Robineau? Killed half a dozen of his herders? Would that*

16

have been any better?

He shook his head savagely. For most of his twenty-six years he had gone with satisfaction from one task to another, finishing them and promptly forgetting them. Spring this year had changed all that. Now he seemed no longer able to forget the things that were past. It was almost as though some instinct told him the Robineau affair was not finished. It was almost as though some inner cautiousness warned him that Howie Frye's vitriolic hatred could not be lightly dismissed.

Yet what could Robineau do to hurt him? What could Howie do? Resolutely he pushed his black uneasiness to the back of his mind and stepped along the walk towards the hotel.

Rose Frye stood at her hotel window which was a bay window, jutting conveniently into the street to give her an excellent view of both sides of Main Street along its entire length. She stared uneasily down into it now and saw Howie standing between two buildings across from Stoddard's. She saw Mart ride in from the edge of town, thinned a little perhaps from the rigors of roundup, tired, dirty, slumping slightly in his saddle. Her heart quickened at the sight of him. She did not begrudge him the lift of a drink or two, for she knew that he would not stay long.

She was turning from the window, unconsciously smoothing her hair, when she saw Howie detach himself from his place of concealment and cross the street towards the saloon. Now the reason for her vague uneasiness became apparent to her, for it increased sharply at Howie's seemingly harmless move. Rose Frye knew Howie. She had grown up as his daughter. She knew his deviousness, knew as well that none of his actions was aimless. She knew that he hated Mart with a vicious intensity, and she even knew why.

But how could she tell Mart the reason for Howie's hatred?

Even yet it seemed incomprehensible to Rose, even yet it seemed like a terrible nightmare, something which had not really happened, which could not really happen. She was beginning to feel afraid, afraid of the man she had called "Father" as long as she could remember. Mart wanted her to marry him and tonight, perhaps, would demand that she answer him one way or the other.

How would she answer? Rose did not know. She saw Mart step out of Stoddard's and knew instantly that Howie had been baiting him. Her smooth face colored with anger. Howie knew the advantage his small stature and his position as Rose's father gave him. He knew it, and he never failed to take advantage of it. Mart would not fight back, being what he was. Pride stirred in Rose, pride in Mart, and all of the old yearning came back to her, the yearning that had lived in her heart since she was twelve, skinny and pig-tailed, peeking through the hedge at Mart as he passed on his way to school.

She had loved him since she was twelve, had lived with the terrible knowledge that he did not return her love, might never return it. She had lain awake so many nights, praying, *O God, let me grow up faster. Keep him for me until I'm big enough for him.*

Now she had him. He lifted his tired and dusty face to her window, and a smile flashed across it, a wide-mouthed, open smile that swept the weariness, the anger, the discouragement from his face as though by magic. Rose waved back, returned his smile, and turned towards the door to wait for the sound of his eager pounding feet on the stairs.

She had him and, loving him, was afraid to keep him. Her answer tonight, if it must be the final one, would be, no. It had to be no. For if Rose married Mart, Howie would kill him. Howie had promised her that, and the concentrated intensity of his promise had made her believe.

18

Tell Mart the whole story, her heart cried out, *and, if he won't believe it, tell Joe Herdic.* But she knew this was only the frantic seeking of her mind for escape from an intolerable predicament. What could Joe Herdic do? Frye had done nothing but make a threat. Herdic's hands would be tied until Howie made his move. Then it would be too late. And only then would it be a case for Joe Herdic, the sheriff. No, there was no way out. Howie had known there would be no way out. That was why he had been so sure.

All the way down the street Mart Joliffe nodded right and left at each man who spoke to him, although he could not muster his usual, cheerful grin. The train pulled noisily into the yellow frame station and began to discharge its passengers and freight while a stream of steam idly hissed beneath it.

Mart looked up at Rose Frye's second-story window in the front of the hotel and raised a hand when he saw her standing there. He grinned at the clerk behind the desk and mounted the steps two at a time, taking then the familiar turn that put him directly before Rose's door.

The door was flung open, and Rose stood waiting, wearing her familiar, warm, full-lipped smile for him. He kicked the door shut behind him and wrapped his arms around her, roughly, hungrily.

The kiss was long, yet Rose's kisses never satisfied him. They only set up a consuming, flaming desire for more. It was Rose who recognized this hunger, who knew it could not forever be put off, and pushed him gently but persistently away.

"You smell like a thousand white-faced steers, a dozen horses, and man-sweat. You need a bath."

Her voice was shaky, and she moved against a table and leaned there so that he would not see the trembling in her knees.

19

"Is that any way to greet a man after he's been gone six weeks?"

His eyes mocked her, and she could not help laughing.

"You know I don't really care. You could crawl out of a mud hole and wrap your arms around me."

"I'll try it some time."

He stared down at her, turning strangely somber, wishing he had not run into Howie Frye at the saloon. Howie had a way of upsetting him, of spoiling his good, reckless, happy moods.

He said, "Rose, it's time we did something about you and me. It's time for you to stop letting things drift and marry me."

A look of sharp unhappiness shadowed Rose's face. She crossed the room and settled herself nervously on a straight-backed chair.

She was a tall girl, brown eyed, with gleaming, midnight hair. Her skin was flawless ivory. She was beautiful, with the glowing, satin-skinned beauty of a wild mare. She gave the same impression of wildness. She was a bird that could be caught briefly but not held. She poised now on her straight-backed chair as though it were but a brief resting place before she again took flight. Mart felt the uneasiness crawling through his body, felt a new touch of fear. He knew in that instant what her answer would be. He knew, but he could not understand.

He asked in order to postpone her answer: "What the hell's the matter with Howie? Would he feel better about it if we got married?"

She shook her head, and her answer was sharply emphatic. "No."

Mart had a new idea, one that had not occurred to him before.

"Does he think we ought to be married? Is that what's eating him?"

Her smile was wan. "No. That's not it."

"Then what is it? I'm tired of hearing him kick your name around the saloon. I'm tired of having my hands tied when he does. I can't hit him. I can't shut him up without hitting him, and he damned well knows it."

Anger raised his voice, anger he could not seem to control. Rose looked at him with her disturbing, soft eyes.

"Marty, oh Marty, don't let's fight! I haven't seen you for six weeks. Don't let Howie spoil tonight for us."

"Then say you'll marry me." He was growing stubborn and could not seem to stop. "Raoul's an old man. He needs a woman around to look after him. I'm a young man, and I need a woman, too."

"Marty, I don't know. I don't know!" Her voice was a cry.

He came across the room and stood before her. His hand tipped her chin up and he kissed her, slowly, insistently.

"Rose, damn it, aren't you sure?"

She was pale, serious, her eyes wide and still.

Mart straightened, briefly cuddled her cheek with his hand. "Think about it. I'll go get cleaned up."

He strode to the door, tossed her a grin that was less than light hearted, and closed it behind him.

Always before he had been warmed by the certainty that some day Rose and he would be married. He had planned it in his own mind for this very fall, when the heavy summer work would be done, when he would be able to spend some time with her. When you have gone with a girl for more than a year, you get to know her. You don't need her words to tell you how she feels or what her answer will be when you finally put the question to her bluntly and plainly. They had talked about marriage. She had never accepted his teasing pro-

21

posals, but neither had she refused.

Tonight had been different. Something had changed Rose in the six weeks he had been away on roundup. Another man? Mart scowled. He didn't think so.

He was half afraid to come out and say, "Rose, give me your answer," but, damn it, they couldn't go on forever as they had been. A man wanted more from a woman than this. He wanted her companionship all of the time. He wanted her face across his table from him. He wanted her beside him at night.

Mart tried to tell himself that he had been imagining things, that he had imagined the clear look of refusal in Rose's eyes. It was a little easier to convince himself here in the busy lobby of the hotel, yet deep within him he knew he had made no mistake.

He was in a black mood, scowling, bitter. In this country he was a powerful man. Yet he was not powerful enough, he told himself, to take the one thing he wanted most. He was not rich enough to buy it, either — he would never be rich enough.

Born to cattle and the open range, these things had become his life. Never pretentious, never loving wealth for its own sake, he had only managed what Raoul handed him to manage. His scowl deepened. His thoughts had returned unwillingly to Robineau and Robineau's sheep. Why couldn't a man ever forget? Why must he go on forever with this guilty feeling, this feeling that nudged him continually with its unpleasant pressure?

Viciously he kicked the hotel door open and stepped onto the verandah. The sun was down, and over the town lay October's evening haze, compounded of wood smoke, dust, and the earth's light moisture, these things held close to the ground by the weight of chilling upper air. The stores along Main Street were closing, and the street was briefly busy with townspeople walking leisurely towards home. Mart rubbed at the stubble on his face.

A buckboard rattled along Main from the depot, bearing beside old Sherman Dawson, the driver, a fashionably dressed, tiny, red-haired woman. Another time Mart would have given her beauty a brief, passing glance and no more. Yet tonight, feeling the dissatisfaction Rose had stirred in him, feeling, too, a puzzled resentment he searched this woman's face with warm, male interest.

He could not have said definitely what it was about her that impressed him the most. Perhaps it was the very obvious fright that widened her large, cool eyes. Perhaps it was the determined set of her red lips. At any rate, almost without thinking, he stepped down off the hotel verandah and offered her his hand to alight upon.

She stumbled and fell against him, murmuring, "Oh, I'm sorry. I. . . ."

So small was she, so perfect, that he was all at once over-poweringly conscious of the dusty, dirty clothes he wore, of the stench of horses and cattle that must emanate from him. He loosed her hand as soon as he decently could and strode off across the street towards Johanson's barber shop.

He heard the reedy voice of Dawson behind him. "Ma'am, you get met in style. That there's Marty Joliffe. Him an' his paw own the biggest ranch in this part of the country." He heard the woman's murmuring voice, but not her words. The voice was pleasant — warm. And Mart was surprised to discover that most of his sourness was gone.

Wonder who she is, he thought, and then promptly forgot her in the shouting banter of Tincup's crew that surged noisily out to greet him from the open door of the barber shop.

"He's already got the prettiest girl in town. But is that enough for him? Hell, no, it ain't. Marty, you leave that redhead for some of us handsome men. She deserves better than you."

Mart grinned, lounged in the doorway, and spoke with a mocking edge to his voice. "I told Stoddard I was buying until ten. I guess you boys don't drink, or you'd be over there."

The clumsy, boisterous rush crowded him out of the door, into the street. He watched them go, grinning, then stepped again into the nearly empty barber shop. Johanson — Swede as he was called — was a medium-size, pale man with light, thinning hair and thick-lensed spectacles through which he habitually peered owlishly.

Mart asked, "Got a tub out back that ain't in use, Swede?"

Johanson peered at him then laid aside his razor and led the way to the back room. As backwoods tonsorial parlors went, this was a good one. The back room was partitioned into booths, with a swinging half door on each. An oak tub and a bench furnished each booth, and in the center of the room was a huge, cast-iron stove, red hot, upon which two wash boilers sat, filled with steaming water.

Swede pushed Mart into an empty booth and bellowed in a high, bodiless voice for his helper.

Mart pulled off his boots. The room was steamy, filled with shouted laughter, ribald comment. Mart began to relax. A bull-shouldered oldster named O'Hara came in tipsily, carrying a bucket in each hand which he dumped unceremoniously into the tub. Mart tested the water with one foot.

"Too cold."

O'Hara went back out, grumbling and scowling, and Mart grinned. O'Hara's breath, in these few short moments, had permeated the booth with the sour odor of whiskey. He brought the other bucket of hot water and dumped it in then stood with fists on hips to survey Mart sourly.

"Now I suppose it's too damned hot?"

Mart wiggled his toe in the water. "Just right." He fished

a dollar from his pocket and handed it to O'Hara. "Go over to Stoddard's and buy yourself a pint."

The sourness went out of O'Hara's face, and he turned to go. But he halted at the door and waited expectantly.

Mart grinned. "Oh, by the way. Stop in at the hotel and get my valise, will you? I had Raoul send me down a change of clothes."

Now O'Hara left. This was a sort of ritual, expected by both and never changing. He could as easily have carried the valise over here himself. He shrugged, shucked out of his clothes, and lowered himself gratefully into the scalding water, letting the soreness soak out of his heavily muscled body. He closed his eyes and drowsed, yet upon his relaxed thoughts intruded the two things which always lately seemed to occupy him whenever the pressure of work eased off. Rose Frye and the slaughter of Robineau's sheep.

Until tonight, thoughts of Rose had always been able to counterbalance the unpleasantness of that other thing. Tonight, those thoughts were as torturing as thoughts of Robineau and his sheep. And tonight the vaguest sort of uneasiness touched Mart briefly and went away.

Chapter Three

Howie Frye watched Mart leave the saloon, a sardonic, triumphant smile creasing his thin lips.

Pete Stoddard said loudly, "Never could understand why the good Lord made so many rattlesnakes. What good are they?"

Howie had heard the train whistle and now felt a compulsion to get out of here, to get down to the station. Yet pride would not let him leave without his drink, the ostensible reason for his coming here. He strode over to the bar — skinny, his complexion sallow and unhealthy. He rang a quarter on the bar, and Pete silently slid him glass and bottle.

Howie smiled unpleasantly, his aplomb unshattered by Pete's obviously pointed remark. "Never could understand why the Lord made leeches, either. All they do is suck blood out of the common people."

Pete colored, and Howie laughed.

"Oh, I don't mean you, Pete. I was thinking about the Joliffes. I read in the paper that Robineau blowed his brains out over at Denver. The Joliffes sucked him dry. So he killed himself."

He tossed off his drink, heard the train wail again as it entered the town's outskirts.

Stoddard scowled. "What would you have done, if it had been up to you, met Robineau with open arms? You know damned good and well that if they'd let him stay, their whole range would have been loaded with sheep before the end of the summer. I say they done right, by God. At least Marty rigged it so nobody got killed."

"You figger Robineau would have killed himself anyway?"

"Well, that ain't Marty's fault. He had his chance to get off Tincup grass. He had more chances than I'd've given him."

Howie sneezed. "I'd expect you to stick up for Tincup. You'd starve to death if it wasn't for Tincup."

Pete scowled viciously and clenched his hands. "I wouldn't starve without you. Drink up and get out of here. I don't give a damn if you never come back."

Frye laughed, but he downed his whiskey, wiped his mouth with the back of his hand, and turned towards the door. A lot of men thought being small was a disadvantage. Howie had discovered just the opposite. He got away with a thousand things he could never get away with if he were larger. With a challenging grin he crossed the saloon and stepped out onto the walk.

He had been meeting every train for a week now, covering the fact with his diffident query each time he went to the station: "You got a telegraph message for me? I been expectin' one. Reckon mebbe the booger's too cheap to wire. Guess I'll get a letter instead."

Tonight he was forced to hurry, for the train was already pulling into the station. He saw the small, red-haired woman alight, and then he stepped into the musty station and turned to stare through the window across the narrow platform.

Lucille Robineau had not been the westbound train's only passenger. A man descended behind her from the coach, a man whose eyes were tawny yellow, whose mouth was thin-lipped and inclined to jerk nervously at its corners. He wore a single gun in a holster at his right thigh, a dark broadcloth coat, and pants tucked into his miner's boots. He carried a capacious but obviously nearly empty carpetbag.

Joe Herdic, star gleaming silver against his vest, pushed his shoulder against the station wall and straightened up. He advanced towards the stranger, saying then in his overly smooth and courteous way, "Stayin' over, stranger? The hotel's half way up on Main Street. There's a boardin' house over at the edge of town" — he eyed the frayed sleeves of the stranger's coat — "if you ain't too flush."

He fished in his vest pocket for his sack of tobacco, carefully poured the flaky stuff into a wheatstraw paper, and rolled a smoke, all this while watching the stranger with cool, questioning eyes. He said as he licked the cigarette, "I'm Joe Herdic. I didn't catch your name."

The sheriff was not a big man, nor did he look like a lawman. Yet about his gray eyes was a cool steadiness, an unflinching, calm consideration. He was something of a dude in his dress, wearing fawn-colored trousers, fancy tooled boots, an ivory-handled Colt in a silver-mounted holster.

Wildness flared in the stranger's tawny eyes. His own gaze met Herdic's steadily. "I didn't tell you my name. Do you meet every train that comes through here? Do you question every stranger that steps down onto the platform?"

Herdic smiled with deceptive gentleness. "No, not every one. Just the ones I wonder about."

The stranger let his bag drop to the platform. His right hand seemed to tense slightly. His voice was low, hissing out through a gap in his front teeth. He said: "Do one of two things, Sheriff. Put me back on the train, or let me alone."

Herdic's smooth face lost its smile. "Tough, eh? All right. But this is a peaceful town, friend. I'm here to see that it stays that way. If you so much as. . . ." He shrugged and turned away, but he flung a soft warning over his solid shoulder — "Be careful."

Thick and precise, he walked across the wooden platform, his heels tapping hollowly, and stepped down in the dust of Main. Without looking back, he went uptown, turning in finally at Stoddard's Saloon.

The stranger picked up his carpetbag. He stood for a moment, scowling at the little town which was so much like other little towns he had seen before.

The station door opened and Howie Frye came out. Howie appeared to be reading a telegraph message from a yellow form he held close to his face. He wandered absently to within ten feet of the stranger, keeping his back towards the station, and then his mouth moved cautiously, "You Shanks?"

He raised his eyes and peered at the stranger, as though now seeing him for the first time. The stranger inclined his head. Howie said, very softly, "I'll see you at Stoddard's later."

He crumpled the sheet of yellow paper and stuffed it into his pocket. Then he turned and sauntered slowly up Main.

The stranger spat disgustedly onto the platform. The corners of his mouth jerked nervously. Another rabbit. Another rabbit who was afraid to do his own killing. He scowled. At last he shrugged fatalistically as though realizing that without the rabbits there would be no employment for the wolves, turned, and followed Frye up the dusty street. He was a shabby and small man but exceedingly dangerous for all of that. He did not go as far as Stoddard's, however, for he was ravenously hungry. Instead, he turned in at the hotel.

Down in the cattle pens below town, twelve hundred Tincup steers crowded and bellowed. A long train of cattle cars labored noisily onto the siding beside the pens and, as soon as they got off the main line, the passenger train whistled and puffed out of the station.

Gray dusk dropped over the town, bringing its high-country chill. Out on the benches across the Little Snake a coyote pack yammered and quarreled. Somewhere in town a piano tinkled the refrain "Flow gently, sweet Afton" rather uncertainly. The racket of Tincup's celebrating 'punchers filled Main Street with its uneven murmur.

Just another night, like a thousand that had gone before it. Yet, somehow, this one was different. Joe Herdic at Stoddard's bar felt an odd and unaccustomed tension he could not explain. Mart Joliffe, as he stabled his horse, untied the slicker behind the saddle, got out his Colt and belt, and strapped them on, wondered at the unnamed compulsion that made him do so. Howie Frye, at a small table in a far corner of Stoddard's, could keep neither his feet nor his hands still, and drank more than was usual for him. But, in spite of his nervousness, a gleam that was part triumph and part wicked anticipation shone in his eyes. Only Shanks in the hotel dining room was calm.

Mart Joliffe, shaved and bathed and attired in clean clothes, climbed the stairs to Rose Frye's room with a certain reluctance. It was not usual for him to feel this way after a six weeks' absence from Rose. Usually he was wildly exuberant, impatiently ardent. Tonight, an odd chill possessed him whenever he thought of Rose. He told himself impatiently — *She isn't going to turn you down. What gives you that notion?* — but he found it hard to believe his own assurances. He had sensed something in Rose today, knew as well as though she had told him that something had happened to change their relationship since he had gone on roundup, something over which he had neither control nor influence.

The very fact that he was so sure something had happened had the power to stir unwilling resentment in him, but he fought to control this as he rapped on the panel of her door. She opened it, her eyes troubled, her mouth unsmiling. Mart put his hands on her shoulders and looked steadily into her eyes, knowing at once that this needed to be brought out into the open before it went farther in either of their minds.

He said: "Rose, you know that I love you. I'm pretty sure

you feel the same way about me . . . hell, I know you do. Will you marry me?"

"Oh, Marty!"

She buried her face against his chest. For a moment her shoulders trembled, and then she stood back. The faintest suggestion of moisture lingered in her eyes, yet her lovely mouth was firmed with determination. She took his hands from her shoulders and stepped away from him, then gave her answer in a low, steady voice.

"No, Marty. I won't. I can't."

"Why? Why? What's happened since I've been gone?"

"Nothing. Nothing at all."

He knew she wasn't being honest. He said: "You're not a very good liar."

Rose raised her eyes, looking directly at him. "Nothing has happened since you've been gone." Her lips began to tremble, and she lowered her eyes immediately.

Anger began to grow in Mart. He wanted to shake her. He wanted to shake some sense into her. He asked bitterly: "You found yourself another man?"

"Yes, Marty."

She would not look at him, so it could not have been her eyes that betrayed her. Yet he was sure she was lying. His anger increased. He shrugged. Reason told him that impatience and anger were useless to him in dealing with this. Yet he could not seem to get rid of either.

"You ready to eat?" he asked.

"You're angry, Marty."

"Sure I am. What do you expect? We've been going together for over a year. You haven't found someone else. That's a bum excuse. What's the real reason, Rose?"

"I told you." Her voice was almost soundless.

"All right." He shrugged. "Come on, we'll eat."

"You don't have to take me, Marty. I'll get something later."

"No. Come on."

She picked up a light shawl from the bed. He noticed suddenly how carefully she had dressed herself for him tonight. *Why had she done that? Only to refuse him?* He could feel his bitterness increasing. He guessed no man would ever understand a woman, least of all himself.

He let her precede him through the door and took her arm as they descended the stairs. Her smooth skin was oddly cold, and Mart could feel the chill growing between them and his own defiance at it. This was not his doing, he told himself emphatically, it was not his fault.

But it was his loss. A hollow desolation came over him as he stared at the future — a future without Rose. *What was a man supposed to do, crawl?* He followed her into the hotel dining room and took a table near the far wall. He saw no one, noticed no one, so absorbed was he with his own private misery. Rose seemed unnaturally pale, and she studiously avoided his glance.

Molly Freret threaded her way through the tables and paused behind Mart's shoulder. Rose forced a weak smile. "Hello, Molly."

Molly was plump and jolly. Her smooth forehead and her upper lip were beaded with perspiration. She spoke in her loud and throaty voice, "Marty, send your boys in tonight in shifts, will you? This is the damnedest night. Everybody in town must have taken a notion to eat out at the same time. It's been like this for over an hour now."

Mart glanced around, suddenly becoming aware that the place was jammed. He grunted, "Sure, Molly, if it will help."

Molly said briskly, "It will. What'll you two have, beef or pork?"

Rose murmured in her subdued voice, "Beef," and Mart

grunted, "Me, too."

When Molly had gone, he put his elbows on the table and stared hard at Rose. She met his glance defiantly. He muttered, "Rose, there's too damned much between us to ever give it up. Do you want to go on for a while?" He gritted his teeth, for to say now what he had to say was the sharpest kind of torture. "What am I going to do, Rose? How am I going to go on without you?"

For the briefest instant Rose Frye's eyes misted, and she blinked them, hard. Her eyes showed him a flash of her naked eagerness, and then even this was gone, leaving only a cold core of refusal, a core of hardness he did not know she possessed.

She shrugged her beautiful shoulders and said resignedly, "We can go on if you want. But it will make no difference. I'll never marry you, Marty."

Desperately she wished she could tell him. She wished she could tell him of the years she had followed him around Cedar City, hoping with quiet desperation that he would notice her. She wanted to tell him how her heart had pounded, of the sharp and bitter ecstasy she felt when his eyes chanced to fall upon her. She wanted to show him the bitter jealousy that had raged in her when she saw him with one of the town's older girls at the Saturday dances in the Odd Fellows Hall. She had loved Mart for as long as she could remember. She loved him still but, if she married him, she would be killing him.

Molly Freret brought their dinner and set it before them. Molly stared penetratingly at one, then the other, then finally asked doubtfully, "You two spattin'?"

"Stop it, Molly!" Rose's voice was unnaturally sharp.

Molly Freret shrugged, raised the hem of her apron to mop her streaming forehead. She grumbled, "Well, it ain't none of my business, I guess," ducked her head and went on.

Rose bent forward to eat, but the food was tasteless, like dry cotton in her mouth. A sense of loss, of life slipping out of her fingers, obsessed her. She looked at Mart, but he would not raise his head.

Depression and hopelessness, greater than she had ever felt before, turned her eyes slack and dull, turned her thoughts dull, too. Over her entire being spread a new feeling of apprehension, of desperate uneasiness, as though tonight death waited in the streets for someone — for someone she loved — for Marty.

Chapter Four

Shanks came out of the hotel and stood on the verandah, picking his yellowed teeth idly with a sharpened match. A crisp October night had settled in the streets while he was eating, and now lamps winked all along Main in the windows of the few stores that remained open this late and in the houses at Main's upper end.

Most of the townspeople were at supper, and the street was nearly deserted. Before Stoddard's Saloon horses bearing Tincup's brand were racked solid. An early drunk weaved back and forth from walk to walk, singing in a low and indistinguishable voice. Uptown a dog barked ceaselessly.

Shanks was watching for Joe Herdic and saw him saunter at last from the saloon, cross Main, and enter his office. Shortly thereafter a lamp threw its feeble rays against the window, illuminating the painted legend.

Sheriff's Office — Jail

Shanks stepped down off the walk then and made his way upstreet towards Stoddard's. The doors of the saloon were open to the chill night air, and smoke and sour whiskey fumes drifted out, visible, almost tangible, in their acrid strength.

The place was packed. Shanks did not immediately see Howie Frye, and so he moved gently through the crowd, diffident, careful to jostle no one. He knew the temper of these payday 'puncher crowds. He knew that they were usually quarrelsome, itching for a fight. He knew as well that the quarrelsome ones would always seek a stranger for their opponent, since tomorrow there would be no need for apology to a stranger, while a friend was different.

He reached the bar eventually, found it full, and waited patiently for a space to open up. Standing this way, he felt a touch against his arm, heard a murmured, cautious voice.

"Get your drink and come around to the alley. I want to talk to you."

Shanks's face twisted, and the corners of his mouth twitched. He looked around, but Frye was gone, lost in the crowd. A careful one, this — a very careful man. Well, he had met a good many careful ones along the kind of trails his sort traveled.

Still he waited, determined to have his drink. After a few moments a narrow space at the bar opened up, and he moved into it. Pete Stoddard slid a bottle and glass towards him, saying, "It's on Mart Joliffe, friend. He's buying until ten."

Shanks rang a quarter down on the bar. "I pay for my own," he said shortly and ignored Stoddard's unfriendly stare. He drank the one and poured the second. He drank that and wiped his mouth with the back of his hand. Then he turned and again made his slow and careful way through the crowd.

On the boardwalk, in the dim glow from the saloon window, he paused and idly shaped a cigarette. He put his shoulder against the saloon wall and smoked it thoughtfully. As he moved away, he arced the stub into the street.

Almost immediately upon leaving the saloon, he entered the darkness that shrouded the rest of Main, and here he increased his gait. At the corner he turned and again at the alley.

Those glowing, tawny eyes could apparently see in the dark, for he threaded his way along the alley silently, avoiding piles of rubbish and tin cans with no missteps until he came to the back door of the saloon.

36

Frye's voice whispered softly out of the shadows. "I'm over here."

"What do you want? What's the story?"

"I want a man shot. Not killed, mind you . . . just shot. You pretty good at hittin' whatever you shoot at?"

"Never had no complaints before," said Shanks laconically. A short warning of suspicion traveled through him. "What makes you think I'll do something like this?"

"I heard that you would." Something rabbit-like quavered in Frye's voice, and then it was gone. "What'd you come for then? You must've known what was in the wind. A man don't travel three hundred miles for. . . ."

Shanks interrupted. "All right. All right. What's his name, and what does he look like? Where do you want him shot?"

He thought he knew the pattern of this now. Someone had been messing with this Frye's wife. He wanted the man disabled, so's he'd let the woman alone, but he didn't want him killed. Shanks shrugged. Damned if he blamed the woman, whoever she was, for wanting something better than Frye.

"Mart Joliffe is the man. Big man. Pale blue eyes, big solid teeth. A young man." A sort of vicious pleasure colored Frye's tone, and Shanks snickered softly. Frye continued, "I want his knees shattered, both of 'em. I want him so's he'll never walk again. I want him in a wheel chair."

"He carry a gun?"

"Damned seldom."

"How much is it worth to you to cripple this Joliffe?"

"Two hundred?"

"Three. And a horse and saddle."

Shanks was hard, callous. He killed for pay, with no questions asked about who was right and who was wrong. But this Frye, the apparent intensity of Frye's hatred, put an odd coldness at the base of his spine.

Frye hesitated. Finally he said reluctantly, "All right."

"How about the horse?"

"There's a sorrel stabled at the livery barn that's mine. He's a good pony, and I hate to part with him. But he'll get you away if you have to run."

Shanks agreed, "All right. Write out a bill of sale for him."

"How do I know you'll do the job? How do I know you won't take the money and the horse and run?"

There was a sudden, ominous silence in the alley.

Frye spoke hastily, "All right. All right. No offense. But I can't write here. It's too dark. I'll be on the hotel verandah with it in fifteen minutes."

Shanks held out his hand. Frye dropped the money into it, fifteen gold double-eagles. Shanks counted them absently and dropped them into his pocket. "All right. Where's Joliffe now?"

"At Stoddard's. Getting drunk. He oughtn't to give you any trouble." Frye chuckled.

Shanks retraced his careful way down the alley and a few moments later emerged on Main. He crossed over and walked slowly towards the livery stable across from the depot.

Checking these small details was part of his defensive armor. He could remember one time when his employer had waited until he had done his job and then had ambushed him at the place where his getaway horse was tied. He smiled a little. He had left two bodies behind him in that particular town.

He passed the sheriff's office, but Joe Herdic, his head buried in paper work, did not even look up. A tow-headed kid of about fourteen sat at a desk in the tiny stable office, playing solitaire.

Shanks asked: "Frye have a sorrel here?"

"Sure. Why?"

"I want to see him. Frye said he'd sell."

"All right."

38

The kid shuffled through the cards in his hand, laid down two face up instead of three. He played the queen from the top and then the seven.

Shanks said: "That's cheating."

The kid looked at him self-consciously. "You wasn't supposed to notice." He laughed, got up, and ran a hand through his long hair. "The horse is out here." He opened the stable door.

Shanks looked at the sorrel, a big gelding with plenty of staying power. Not a fancy horse but one to carry a man in rough country. Shanks's opinion of Frye rose slightly. Still, Frye had as much to lose by Shanks's being caught as Shanks had himself.

The gunman said: "Saddle him up. Tie him out on the street. I'll have a bill of sale when I come after him."

"Sure."

The kid's face in lantern light was curious, but the stamp that was on Shanks turned him unsure and kept him silent. Shanks went back out of the stable through the big double door, and the kid began to saddle the horse.

From here the lights of the town were dimmed by the smoky haze that lay in the streets. Shanks walked uptown slowly. There were times, even yet, when he felt a fleeting regret at the way his life had gone. This was one of them, and he didn't know why. Unless it was the smell of fall, so sharp and clear tonight, the haze that lay in the streets, the sound of that damned piano that stirred some unnamed memory from out of the past.

Then the corners of his mouth twitched again, and he climbed the hotel steps. Frye was a shadow in the depths of the deserted verandah. He handed a paper to Shanks, and the gunman read it carefully in the dim light. More of his defensive armor. No one caught him riding a strange horse without a bill of sale to prove ownership if he could help it.

Satisfied, he asked: "Still in the saloon?"

"Yeah."

"I'll wait. Give me a wave when he comes out."

Shanks slipped down off the verandah, crossed the street, and lost himself in the shadows.

Lucille Robineau was somewhat too young fully to realize the power which her striking beauty gave her, although she had seen some evidence of this power during the past summer, working as a waitress in Denver. She had seen further evidence of it during her trip to Cedar City on the train. She had no concrete plan for revenge against Mart Joliffe, other than the certainty that, if she put herself in the same town with him, something was bound to occur to her, some opportunity was bound to present itself.

Since her mother's name had been Roberts, and since Robineau would be a name too well known, too widely remembered, she registered at the town's hotel as Lucille Roberts. Now she sat at a tiny table in a far corner of the large hotel dining room, unnoticed, and watched Rose Frye and Mart Joliffe eat their dinner and quarrel.

Hatred had become an obsession with Lucille. All in the course of one short summer her father had been robbed of the accumulation of a lifetime. She herself had been reduced to penury and, as though this were not enough, she had been cast adrift by her father's death in a world with which she was untrained to cope. She blamed Mart Joliffe for her father's death just as much as she would had it been he who actually pulled the trigger of the Navy revolver.

With eyes that reflected this naked hatred, she studied the big man. He was tall, just over six feet, and he was solidly built, so that he must have weighed close to a hundred and eighty. His face, deeply tanned, was bony and hard planed, with high cheekbones that made him look almost as though he had Indian blood. Perhaps he had. The Joliffes were a pioneer family of French descent who had followed the tide of conquest westward for a hundred years.

His hair was black, crisp and coarse, and his eyes below it were pale blue, like the sky on a hot day. His was a singularly arresting face, yet one which could stir nothing but hatred in this tiny, red-haired woman. Perhaps the powerful virility of his face stirred a greater hatred in her than it otherwise would have because it had the power to attract her against her will.

In her mind she marshaled her assets and stacked them against the strength of the man she had to beat. Money was the least of her assets, there being but sixty-seven dollars remaining of the pittance her father had left when he died. Burial costs had been high, and there had been the train fare here, a few small additions to her wardrobe. Her strength was nothing against that of Mart Joliffe. There remained, then, only what beauty she happened to possess, only her woman's body, to be used as weapons. How could these things be used to their best advantage? *In marriage* came her mind's immediate answer to the question.

Then for the present she must make herself forget that she hated Joliffe. She must will her mind to believe she loved him. She must make him aware of her, at once, and after that she must show him only the things in her that a man could love and want. If he so much as sensed that hate festered in her heart, then she was lost.

Though she had never tested the particular attributes which she now needed, Lucille had them in abundance. She was an actress born. She had as well a powerful will, one which could force from her mind and body the obedience it desired.

She had been watching Mart Joliffe coldly, with her hate plainly mirrored in her lovely eyes. Now, as quickly as she decided upon her course of action, all of the coldness left her glance, all of the hate, and there remained only a woman's intense interest in a man, only the helplessness of her attraction to him.

She watched him as he coldly helped the beautiful woman who was with him to her feet, watched him as he followed her from the dining room, looking neither to right nor left. She smiled faintly, for she could tell that Joliffe was very angry, could also discern that he was hurt, even desperately so.

Instinct told her instantly that, if he was angry with this woman he was with, no time could be better than the present for Lucille Roberts to make herself known to him. Therefore, although her dinner was not quite finished, she rose immediately after the two had left and placed herself, standing, near the wide stairway, so that when he descended, she would be unavoidable.

She had sensed that his quarrel with the dark-haired woman was an advantage to herself. She could not realize what a terrifically powerful advantage it was. She could not know that Mart Joliffe had reached a crossroads in his life and was not hesitating at the turn.

As he descended the stairs, anger blazed in his light-blue eyes. For an instant those blazing eyes rested upon her, flickered with recognition. Then she was crossing in front of him, as though she had just then remembered something, so that he had to stop for her, so that for the briefest instant she had his full attention.

Appearing completely preoccupied, completely unaware of his presence, she deviated from her course the slightest bit and felt the contact of their bodies.

"Oh! Pardon me."

She stepped back and looked up at him, smiling apologetically. She made the smile dazzling. She made her eyes warm, made

42

them show him the full extent of her startled interest. Her voice was low and throaty.

"We seem to keep bumping into each other. I'm sorry. It was my fault. I was thinking of something else."

She seemed to realize suddenly that this man was a stranger, to whom she had not been properly introduced. She repeated — "I'm sorry" — in a cooler voice and started to step away.

He caught her arm. He was smiling as she looked up, all of his anger gone.

He said: "I'm not a bit sorry. It's not every day in Cedar City a man can bump into a girl as pretty as you are. I'm Mart Joliffe."

Her eyes remained soft and interested, but they showed him her quick reserve as well.

She answered: "And I'm Lucille Roberts."

"I know."

"How?"

She was genuinely surprised.

"I looked at the register."

Lucille gave him a long, speculative look, lips gently curving.

He asked: "You'll be staying here for a while?"

"Yes."

"Then I'll see you again."

For a long moment he stared at her, his eyes turning strange as though he were seeing not her but someone else. At last he turned and then went striding across the lobby. He banged through the doors and turned upstreet towards Stoddard's Saloon.

Lucille watched the closed door through which he had passed for a moment, her face thoughtful and still. Then she slowly climbed the stairs.

She knew there was a long path to be traveled. Yet she could feel a certain satisfaction. She had at least met the man she was after within hours of her arrival. She had made him notice her.

In the privacy of her room her face hardened. There would be no rules in her coming contest with him. If she ever weakened, which was unlikely, she had only to think of her father, the back of his head blown away. She had only to think of the bones of Robineau's sheep, mouldering at the foot of the rim.

Chapter Five

Drink after drink Mart poured for himself, yet tonight the liquor had no power to bring him forgetfulness, no power to ease his tortured thoughts. This he kept asking himself, *Why? Why? What the devil's got into her?*

He was enraged and wildly jealous as he considered her assertion that there was another man, yet he knew she had been lying about that, knew there was no one else for her. There was no subterfuge in Rose. Her love for him had been one of the steady things, the things he could count upon like the sun rising every morning, like snow in winter and rain in summer.

Morose, sour, he scowled at the brown bottle before him, now more than half empty. When he had first come into the saloon, Tincup's 'punchers had been friendly and jocular with him. His responses had been surly, and now, at last, they let him alone to drink in solitary misery. The hubbub and uproar in the saloon increased as the hours passed, but Mart did not notice and, finally unable to find release from his thoughts in liquor, he walked carefully to the door and stepped out into the night.

Cold air felt good against his damp brow. Swaying slightly, he rolled a cigarette. He stared hard at the second story window of the hotel, the room which Rose Frye occupied, his mind still wrestling futilely with the enigma of her refusal. Then he headed downstreet, toward the river, toward the livery barn where he had stabled his horse.

Darkness closed about him as soon as he left the glow that

lay in the street before the saloon. He crossed the street, remaining in darkness, and there, before the sheriff's office, paused again to stare regretfully at the hotel.

A light still glowed in Rose Frye's room, but the shades were drawn and billowed slightly into the room with evening's cool breeze. He made a high, broad shape against the light in the sheriff's window. Shadow hid the pain in his face, hid the awful indecision. If he went out of town tonight, Rose would be lost to him forever, for his earlier words, his parting words, had been harsh and uncompromising. If he could unbend, if he could go over there now and humble himself before her, then there was still a chance, a chance that he could discover the reason behind her adamant refusal and, knowing the reason, could change her decision.

He went back over, in his mind, the things that had happened in the past year and a half. For one thing, Rose had moved from her home with Howie to the hotel. He thought he had detected a change in her then, yet it had been, and still was, a thing upon which he could not put a finger — more a feeling than a certainty.

Even then, immediately following her move to the hotel, there had been little noticeable change in her attitude towards him. If anything, she had been a little more affectionate, a little more anxious for the assurance his love could give her. Why, then, the abrupt about-face?

He could not help thinking that he had the ingredients for the solution of the puzzle, yet he could not fit them together. His mind was fuzzy tonight from liquor, from the strain of trying to break his puzzlement. He shrugged slightly, glanced once more at her window. He thought he saw the shade move but decided it must have been a vagary of the wind. He turned and, walking beneath the broad awnings that stretched out over the walk, continued on towards the stable.

46

He had consumed a prodigious amount of whiskey tonight, yet it now affected him not at all, and the only indication of its presence within him was the faint headache that throbbed above his right eye — that and the slight dulling of his senses, at all other times so very sharp.

He did not hear the faint scuff of a miner's boot on the walk behind him, nor the faint click that the hammer on Shanks's gun made as he thumbed it back. But he heard Rose Frye's frantic scream as it crashed along the silent street.

"Marty! Look out!"

He whirled towards the hotel. She stood in the bay window, the shade thrust aside, and now she screamed again.

"Marty! Behind you!"

She had been watching him, even as he had watched the shade-drawn window of her room, yet he had no time for this realization now. As his eyes dropped from Rose's window, they caught a blur of movement on the hotel verandah, as Frye moved across it and took his place at the rail. A voice behind him rasped intemperately.

"Damn you, stand still!"

He whirled towards it, stepping aside, still puzzled, still bemused. He did not yet realize what the danger was, nor from what quarter it threatened, yet this voice gave him something to act upon. It was a strange voice, one Mart knew he had never heard before. It had a sort of hissing quality, as though the speaker had a gap in his teeth.

He saw the flare of a revolver muzzle spit seconds before the roar of the gun clapped against his ears, and his hand immediately started its swift, unerring way towards his holster. Uneasiness, upon which he could not put a finger, had compelled him to wear his gun tonight. Now he was briefly and desperately glad that he had.

A post that supported the awning, catching a glow of light

from the hotel across the street, caught Mart's eye, and he leaped to put himself behind it. A bullet tore a shower of splinters from the post, briefly startling to Mart because it struck so low. Another bullet struck the post, equally low, making its dull, whacking sound. Mart raised his own gun but, before he could bring it to bear, the ambusher's fourth bullet slammed against his leg with the force of a mule's hind hoof and ripped it out from under him.

He went sprawling to the walk and rolled immediately off, raising his own gun against the shadowy form there against the wall.

Joe Herdic's door slammed open, and Joe pounded down the walk toward him, gun in hand. The hotel across the street erupted half a dozen of the curious, and Stoddard's Saloon spewed Tincup 'punchers from its door in a solid stream.

Mart got off his shot and heard a hoarse groan as the bullet found its mark. Yet again that shadowy fisted revolver in the ambusher's hand flashed, and the last shot, fired in desperation, entered Mart Joliffe's side, brought its searing pain, its immediate lassitude, and then unconsciousness.

Shanks's gun clicked in his hand, the hammer falling on an empty chamber. He cursed and fumbled frantically in his belt for more shells. Herdic, the sheriff, was a looming, rapidly approaching form on his right, and angling across the street behind Herdic came a full dozen Tincup 'punchers, some of them carrying guns.

Down street, Shanks could see the railroad station agent standing on the platform, peering into the street. The livery barn, across from the station, had a shadowy figure before it, probably the tow-haired kid that cheated at solitaire. Tied to the rack before the stable was the sorrel horse. If he could reach that horse. . . .

But Shanks had Mart's bullet in his thigh. Holding on to the wall with his left hand, he put weight experimentally on the wounded leg. It gave out from under him and he fell against the wall.

Well, this was it. A man traveled the crooked trails for years, taking worse risks than he had tonight a dozen times every year, and he always came out of it. It was some little thing that tripped him up. Like Frye's insistence that Joliffe be crippled. That was the thing that had tripped Shanks up tonight. He could have killed Mart with one shot. But the damned fool kept moving his legs, and Shanks had not been able to shatter them in this kind of light, moving as they were and partially protected by the shelter of that damned, unforeseen post.

Pure rage had made him put his last bullet into Joliffe's body. Pure anger and bitter resentment. Now he knew he would have done better to save it for Herdic.

He thumbed shells into the Colt's loading gate — one, two, three. He fumbled the fourth, and it ticked against the boardwalk.

Herdic's shot crashed out, slammed into his body, drove him viciously backwards. He recovered, closed the gun's loading gate. Three would have to do. But he forgot one thing, as used was he to loading the gun fully. He forgot the empty chambers which would have to pass under the hammer before the gun would fire.

He lifted the gun, centered on Herdic's body, and thumbed back the hammer. The gun clicked. Desperately, Shanks tried again, and again the gun clicked. Herdic was but half a dozen paces from him now. Shanks thumbed back the hammer a third time.

It was then that Herdic's bullet took him, tearing into his shirt pocket and his chest beneath. There was the briefest instant of shocked realization that a lethal bullet had at last struck him, and then he was falling. The harsh sounds of the street faded in his consciousness. Then the light. Shanks was dead.

Joe Herdic viciously toed the still form of Shanks. The killer's body was yielding and soft. Herdic knelt and snatched the gun from the killer's hand, flinging it into the street. He came to Mart Joliffe's inert body and yelled out.

"Doc! One of you run for Doc!"

A Tincup 'puncher raised a querulous voice. "Who the hell is it? What'd he have against Marty?"

These were the questions Herdic had been asking himself. He had recognized the killer as the seedy, dour man he had warned at the railroad station earlier this evening. He had known the breed even then, had recognized the plain stamp of viciousness the man had worn. The only thought that touched him was brief, but sure — *Robineau's work.*

Rose Frye came running across the street from the hotel in bare feet and nightgown, a woolen wrapper clutched about her, silently running like a terrified doe. She shoved Joe Herdic aside, so that he staggered in the dusty street, and flung herself down beside Mart Joliffe.

Tears coursed down her cheeks, silent, terrible tears. A circle formed close about Mart's body, and Herdic bawled, "Break it up, damn you! He ain't dead yet. Who went after Doc?"

A dozen subdued Tincup voices murmured, "Floyd went. Here he comes now, with Doc."

Rose Frye stood up to give Doc Saunders room beside Mart. Another woman, the one who had come in on the train this afternoon, came up beside her, and Herdic heard her ask, "Is he dead?"

Rose's voice was not her own. "No. He isn't dead."

Herdic could see the newcomer's lips moving in silent prayer.

Oh, God, not yet, please not yet.

Herdic watched as Doc Saunders made his hasty examination by the flickering light of a lantern someone had showed the foresight to bring. He stood up, grunting.

"Leg bone. Above the knee. Another one in the ribs. Dunno what it done. Pick him up carefully, boys, about six of you. Hold him level and don't move him no more'n you got to. Bring him over to the hotel."

He snapped his bag shut and waddled on his short legs towards the hotel, puffing. Herdic swiveled his glance back to the inert form of the killer and saw Howie Frye standing over him, looking down.

Herdic could not account for the fleeting suspicion that stirred in him, but he was somehow sure that, had he turned an instant sooner, he would have seen Frye kneeling over the killer's body.

Floyd Timmons stood spraddle-legged before Joe Herdic now and shoved his belligerent jaw forward.

"Who the hell is that one? What's he doin' in Cedar City? What's he got against Marty?"

Herdic replied snappishly, "I don't know a damned bit more about it than you do. That little guy came in on the train this evening. He hadn't done nothin' then. Was I supposed to run him out because he didn't look good?"

"You're the sheriff, ain't you? Is Tincup supposed to watch your blasted railroad station?"

Joe Stoddard pushed between them. He yelled, "Hey! Hey! It ain't nobody's fault, Floyd. We all like Marty, and we're all sore about this. But there ain't nothin' t' be gained by callin' names."

Floyd Timmons's wide shoulders sagged. He muttered, "Sorry, Joe."

"Sure. Forget it. I should have put him back on the train. I'd 'a' done it, too, if I'd known he was after Marty."

He stepped up on the walk and went over to where the killer's body sprawled. He heard Cassius Riley, the fifteen-year-old, tow-headed kid that watched the stable evenings say to Howie Frye, "Did he buy your sorrel, Mister Frye? He was down there just a few minutes ago, big as life, lookin' at your horse."

Howie grunted irritably. "What the hell you talkin' about, Cassius? I never seen him before in my life."

Cassius looked nonplused. "Well, he said your horse was for sale, and he wanted to look at him. He said to saddle him and tie him out front, and he'd bring a bill of sale from you when he came after him."

Something troubled Herdic, and suddenly he knew what it was. He said: "Howie, you was at the station when the train pulled in, wasn't you?"

"Sure," perhaps a little defiantly. "Is that any crime? I been expectin' a wire from Denver."

"You get it?"

"No."

Herdic mused, "There ain't half a dozen passengers get off at Cedar City every month. Don't seem natural you wouldn't notice the ones that got off tonight, seein' as you was down at the station. You see that girl that got off tonight?"

"Sure."

"But you didn't see this one?"

"I didn't say I didn't see him. Sure I saw him. But I didn't know who he was."

Herdic thought Frye was nervous. He persisted. "But just now you told Cassius you never saw this man before in your life."

The overly prominent Adam's apple below Frye's chin wobbled a couple of times as he swallowed. He began to get red. "Sheriff, damn you, what are you tryin' to say? If you've got anything on your mind, by God, you get it out but don't stand there skirtin' around it."

Herdic shrugged. "Don't get on the prod, Frye. I'm just trying to find out what this is all about."

"Well, I don't know what it's all about. So don't be pryin' around me with your damned questions."

Herdic scowled at him. He knelt beside the body and began a systematic search of the man's pockets. Tobacco and cigarette papers in the two upper vest pockets, matches and change in the two lower ones. A plug of chewing tobacco in the shirt pocket, damp with the man's blood.

Suddenly Herdic halted. If he had needed proof that Frye had rifled this man's pockets, he had it now. Proof enough for his own certainty anyway, if not proof that would hold up in court, for one of Shanks's side pants pockets was half turned inside out. The other pants pocket, on the left side, had a big hole in it and was empty.

Herdic stood up.

Timmons asked: "What'd you find?"

"Not a damned thing." Herdic pointed to the handful of small change where he had laid it on the boardwalk. "That's every dime he had. Don't look like business is very good for killers these days. One thing I'm sure of, though. He didn't shoot Marty for nothing. He was paid for it. So where's the money? Maybe he didn't get it all when he agreed to do the job, but he sure as hell got part of it. I know how these guys work. And another thing. He must've been figurin' on buyin' Frye's horse. How was he goin' to pay for it?"

Howie suggested in his whining voice, "Maybe that was just a stall. Maybe he was going to steal him. I'm glad you killed him, Joe. I reckon you saved me a hundred dollars' worth of horse by killin' him."

Joe grunted dryly, "Glad to do you a favor any time, Howie."

He surveyed the thinning crowd. "How about a couple of you carrying him into my office for tonight? I guess we can wait 'til tomorrow to plant him."

He had thought that Robineau must be behind this attempt at Mart Joliffe's life. Now he was not so sure. He turned again to Howie Frye, a little uncertain but determined for all of that. He asked: "Howie, what'd you think of Mart Joliffe? You don't like him much, do you? Why?"

"It ain't no damned secret that I don't like Mart. Everybody in town knows it."

"You had a run-in with Mart down at Stoddard's this afternoon, didn't you?"

"So what if I did?"

"Pete says you threatened to kill Mart."

Howie laughed. "It ain't the first time. Pete tell you what else I told him?"

"What was that?"

"That I wanted him down on the ground in front of his damned throne. That I wanted to see him broke and hungry. That I wanted him crawling by the time I killed him."

Herdic felt contaminated by the virulence of Frye's hate. He murmured wonderingly, "What'd Mart ever do to you, Howie? What'd he do to make you hate him like that? He's been going with Rose. Everybody figures they're going to get married. That'd make you Mart's father-in-law."

Howie fairly screeched at him, "They ain't goin' to get married! By God, they ain't! Damn you, Herdic, you say that once more, and I'll kill *you!* You hear that? Sheriff or not, I'll kill you!"

For an instant Joe Herdic was too startled to speak. Then, at last, the nervousness and the fear that sane people feel in the presence of the insane came over him. He grunted, "Go home, Howie. You're nuts." He backed off and repeated, "By God, I believe you are crazy."

Chapter Six

Rose left the bickering men behind, following the six Tincup 'punchers who carried Mart. She followed them up the stairs, her face contorting every time they unavoidably twisted or jarred Joliffe's body. They carried him into an empty room and placed him on his back on the bed. Doc shooed them out, irritably and impatiently, and closed the door.

A moment later he poked his head out, saying, "Get me a quart of whiskey. Quick."

One of the 'punchers took the stairs running and, after what seemed an eternity but could not have been more than a minute or two, he came back. Again the door closed.

Rose waited. She put her hands over her face, and the tears welled out of her eyes and flowed unchecked across her cheeks. Howie Frye had not fired the shots into Mart tonight, but he had directed them. Howie's gold had hired the gunman. Rose knew this as surely as she knew that Howie would try again.

Oh, God, she prayed. *Let him live. I'll go away, and then Howie will have no reason for killing him.*

She was trembling, partly from cold, partly from her horror and fear. Lucille Roberts came to her and timidly touched her arm.

"You're cold. It will be a while yet. Why don't you get some clothes on? I'll go downstairs and get you some coffee."

Rose looked at her gratefully.

"All right."

She went down the hall to her room and closed the door behind. She walked to her window and stared down into the street. The body of the killer still lay where it had fallen, and before the sheriff stood a defiant Howie Frye. Rose felt a quick stab of hope. Perhaps the sheriff entertained the same suspicions about Howie that Rose did. Perhaps he would be able to prove them where Rose could not. Perhaps he could make Howie pay for his crime.

The longer she watched, the dimmer her hope became. Howie stood defiantly, not at all as a man would stand who was unsure of himself. At last Herdic turned away from him.

With tears standing in her eyes, Rose slipped out of her nightgown and began to dress. She was slipping on her shoes as Lucille knocked at the door. Rose raised a pleading, questioning glance, but Lucille shook her head.

"He's still in there with the doctor. Here, drink this coffee. It will warm you up and make you feel better."

Rose smiled gratefully. She gulped the scalding coffee and then stood up.

"Do you mind if we go back? I'm so worried."

"Of course not."

They went out into the dimly lighted hallway. Joe Herdic had come upstairs and now squatted with his back against the wall, waiting. Floyd Timmons was there, too, and Stoddard, and a few of Tincup's older 'punchers, men who had known Mart as a boy.

At last the door was flung open. Doc spoke instinctively to Rose.

"I think he'll make it, honey. I think he will. The bone in his leg wasn't shattered . . . just broke. The other bullet got a couple of ribs an' shaved a lung. But he'll be here quite a while." He seemed to realize suddenly that he was holding the quart whiskey bottle in his hand. He muttered, "Used this for an antiseptic. Guess I could use some inside of me now." He took a long drink and then passed the bottle to Floyd.

Abruptly every bit of Rose's strength went out of her. Dizziness mounted to her brain until the corridor and the people in it swam crazily before her eyes. She could feel herself falling, and then Floyd Timmons's strong arms were about her, scooping her up.

He carried her down the hall to her own room and laid her on the bed. Through a haze of half consciousness, Rose heard the soft, sweet tones of Lucille Roberts saying, "Go on now. All of you. I'll look after her."

She heard Floyd's gruff, "Good girl. Thanks." She heard the door close. Then the woman was hovering over her, helping her out of her clothes, laying a cool cloth to her forehead.

Lucille asked softly, sympathetically, "Are you and Mister Joliffe going to be married?"

"No." Rose's voice was low, without expression. No, she could not marry Mart, could never marry him. Not while Howie Frye lived. She said: "I'm going away tomorrow. I'm going away."

A sort of daze seemed to come over her, a daze in which all things were vague and unreal. Her mind contemplated the empty years. She sat up while Lucille helped her into her nightgown, but she did not seem to see the girl. She simply stared at the wall.

Lucille asked worriedly, "Rose, are you all right?"

Rose nodded and lay back on the bed. Lucille pulled the covers up to her chin and turned towards the door, "Go to sleep."

Again Rose nodded. But as the door closed behind Lucille, a great shudder ran through Rose's body, and at last she began to cry.

In mid-morning on Friday a long freight pulled out of Cedar City loaded with Tincup's steers and commenced the long, puffing drag towards the Continental Divide. Rose Frye stood at the bay window of her room, looking down into the dusty street, looking eastward and watching the line of brick-red, slatted cars crawl out of sight.

She saw the gleaming, yellow-wheeled buckboard that was Raoul Joliffe's private vehicle come rolling into town behind a team of shining bays — high-stepping, high-spirited animals that Raoul had shipped in from Kentucky for this especial purpose.

She saw Raoul's stiff, ramrod figure behind the reins, and Floyd Timmons's bulkier shape beside him, straight-sitting with nervousness over the old man's reckless driving.

Raoul pulled up with a flourish before the hotel, cursing the team in his vigorous voice, "Whoa, dammit, whoa. Get down, Floyd, and take the reins. Whoa!"

Floyd got down and caught the bridles of the horses. One of them reared. Both were excited, lathered, and hot. Raoul climbed from the seat, only a little stiff. He made a tall, bony, but regal figure. His flowing mustaches were snowy white, accentuating by their whiteness his dark, ancient skin. His lips were sensitive, smooth, and firm. His nose was hawk-like. His was the face of an Indian chief, save for the eyes, pale blue like Mart's and fierce as an eagle's. An old scar slashed upwards across his cheek from the point of his nose, giving him a certain savage look.

Rose could not help thinking, wistfully, *Mart will look like that when he gets old.* Then she thought of Mart as she had seen him this morning, white and wan beneath the blankets of his bed, his face drawn and twisted with pain.

Raoul fished his cane from behind the buckboard seat and stalked up the hotel steps, tall and gaunt, muttering savagely, "Hell! They'd let the boy die afore they'd send for me! By God, next time. . . ."

He went into the door, out of Rose's sight, still muttering. Rose could not help smiling faintly. She liked Raoul and knew he liked her.

She could tell Raoul the reason for Howie's hate, could tell him that Howie was behind Mart's shooting last night. She knew very certainly what Raoul would do if she did. He'd go down in the street, find Howie, and kill him, kill him as he would kill a gray wolf on Tincup's range, and with no more compunction.

Then Joe Herdic would have to arrest him. He'd lay in Cedar City's dirty jail until the District Court was in session, and after that he would go to the pen in Canyon City to spend the rest of his days like a caged lion. He'd die with his spirit broken. He'd die a senile and helpless old man.

Rose never even considered this course. She couldn't do that to Raoul. She couldn't be the one to start him on the course that would kill his savage grandeur, humble him, and break his heart.

She shrugged bitterly, got her alligator bag out of the closet, and began to pack. Doc Saunders had definitely assured her this morning that Mart would live. There was nothing further, then, to keep her here.

Mart would find someone else. Perhaps Lucille. . . . Rose's face contorted, and tears of pure jealousy welled into her eyes. She dried them fiercely, angrily. This was no way to act.

She was finished at last. She picked up her bag, slung her coat over her arm, and stepped to the door. As she put her hand on the doorknob, someone knocked. Rose opened the door.

Raoul stood in the hall, hatless, his long, white hair framing his dark face.

"Where you goin'?"

"Away. To Denver, I guess."

"Why?"

59

He was blunt, direct. He could make Rose feel very guilty in the way he looked at her, and she could feel defiance rising in her.

She murmured, "Because I want to."

Raoul's eyes narrowed bitterly.

"He's hurt, so now you're runnin' out on him, that it? You ain't woman enough to stick around an' look after him 'til he's well again. Hell, ma'am, I'm glad he didn't marry you. I'm glad he didn't. He's all man. He's. . . ." He stopped, glaring. "He deserves a real woman when he catches one. You ain't it, so I'm glad you're going." His shoulders sagged suddenly. "No, I ain't glad. I'm sorry. What's got into you, Rose? There's somethin' wrong. You're runnin', but you ain't runnin' from Mart. Whyn't you tell me?"

Rose shook her head stubbornly, making her expression cold. She said: "I don't love Mart. There's someone else." She knew that if Raoul didn't leave her that she would break down. She made her voice sharp, cruel. "Go away. I'm busy. I haven't got time to talk to you."

He scowled at her fiercely for an instant then turned and stamped back down the hall to Mart's room. For a long moment Rose stood quite still, her face drained of color, her eyes dull and still. Then she was hurrying, down the stairs, past the desk, and into the street.

An hour later, when the eastbound train puffed out of town, Rose was on it, staring back at the diminishing, ugly shapes of Cedar City.

Mart recovered consciousness only briefly and at widely spaced intervals during that first week. During these lucid intervals he was intensely aware of Rose's absence and at last, during one of them, he recalled all the events of Thursday night, the break with Rose, the brooding afterwards in the

60

saloon, the shooting. . . .

Someone laid a soft, cool hand against his brow. He opened his eyes, saw a woman's face above him, looking down. For the briefest instant he thought it was Rose, come back, and that all of his troubled thoughts were over. Then he saw that her hair was red, that her eyes, instead of being a soft, dark brown, were hazel, bordering on green.

She murmured, "Well! So you've come out of it at last? Doctor Saunders said you might today. How do you feel?"

Mart made a wry, weak grin. "Terrible. What time is it?"

"Mid-afternoon." She looked at her watch. "Three o'clock to be exact. The day is Wednesday. It has been almost a week since you were shot."

"And you've been here all that time?"

She looked away. "There wasn't anyone else. Oh, I suppose your father could have got one of the women in town to look after you, but. . . ." She hesitated.

"But what?"

Lucille was blushing. She raised her eyes defiantly. "I wanted to do it."

Mart stirred and grimaced with pain. "Good of you." His mind groped, rummaged around in the things he remembered. After a while he asked, "Who was it that shot me?"

"A stranger. Nobody in town knew him. He came in on the same train I did. A little man, thin and shabby. The sheriff thinks he was hired to kill you."

Mart closed his eyes. "Robineau."

Occupied by his own thoughts, he did not notice the long silence. Finally the girl said, her voice small, "No."

Mart opened his eyes.

"Couldn't be anyone else. What makes you think it wasn't Robineau?"

He wondered at the sudden flush that stained her cheeks.

He wondered at her abrupt confusion.

She said hastily: "I was thinking of something else. Who is Robineau?"

Mart grunted, letting his eyes fall closed again. "Sheepman. He ran a thousand sheep onto Tincup's grass last spring. Wouldn't move off. I ran his sheep off the rim."

He let his thoughts wander, remembering Robineau, recalling that there had been neither hate nor anger in the man but only the bitterness of complete defeat. It seemed strange that Robineau would let the entire summer pass without making a retaliatory move and then, when fall came, send a gunman to kill Mart.

Most of the folks in Cedar City liked Mart. There were a few that didn't, men like Howie Frye, whose hates were incomprehensible and apparently without cause. But he doubted if any of them hated him enough to spend good money trying to get rid of him. It must have been Robineau. It could be no one else.

He asked, his voice weakening, "What happened after he got me?"

"The sheriff shot him."

"Kill him?"

"Yes. Mister Herdic went through all his pockets. He didn't find anything, though, but some tobacco and a little small change. The sheriff says he's keeping the man's gun for you. He thought you'd like to have it for a souvenir."

Mart grinned.

Lucille said, rising: "You sleep now. You've tired yourself out, talking."

Mart nodded. "All right."

He heard the rustling passage to the door, heard it close behind her. His thoughts turned bitter.

So Rose had not even cared enough to stay with him when

he was hurt? He had wanted desperately to ask Lucille where Rose was, where she had gone. He had withheld the question only because of the shreds of pride that were left to him. Yet it was obvious to him now that she was no longer in Cedar City. He could not believe that Rose hated him. He could not believe that if she were in town that she would not have come to see him.

It left but one inevitable conclusion in his mind. Rose was gone out of his life forever. Well, other men had lost the things they loved before this. Life did not stop because of it. Life went on. Mart's life would go on, too.

Raoul was getting old, and Raoul would like to see some grandsons playing in the yard at Tincup before he died.

Mart's thoughts turned to Lucille Roberts. He thought of her for a while, wondered about her. But, as he began to drowse, it was not Lucille's face that hovered in his thoughts. It was Rose's. He went to sleep, bleakly contemplating what his life would be without her.

Chapter Seven

October slipped away. Yellow leaves whirled down Cedar City's dusty streets, driven by November's icy blasts. The high country got its first coat of winter's ermine, light and powdery and soft. Tincup's last roundup brought the remaining cattle off the high plateau. At last, winter set in — in earnest. Day after day the frigid wind howled down Cedar City's main street, driving before it blinding, stinging clouds of drifting snow. Snow piled up, and the weather cleared. The temperature went to twenty below and stayed there, except for a brief, ten-degree climb during each afternoon.

As Martin Joliffe mended, Lucille saw all of the signs of a man's interest and a man's gratitude in him and felt a growing, satisfying contentment. She had quickly seen, immediately following the shooting, that here was a rare opportunity, perhaps a never-to-be-repeated one. As though fate saw fit to deal Lucille a winning hand, Rose, the only one who could have frustrated Lucille's plan, had left.

There were times when Lucille puzzled over this. She puzzled over Howie Frye, Rose's father, and wondered often what lay behind Howie's obvious hatred of Mart. She sensed in Howie an ally, and perhaps her feeling that Howie might some day be useful to her engendered a great deal of her curiosity about the man. It was not natural for a father so to hate the man his daughter loved, particularly when that man was as wealthy as Mart and as well endowed with other admirable characteristics. Discreetly, Lucille inquired about Mart's relationship with Rose, feeling that if there was anything in that which would bear scrutiny, she would hear about it quickly in a town the size of Cedar City. But she heard nothing.

She was very good to Mart, very patient with him. Slowly, very slowly, she allowed the warm, personal interest to creep into her eyes, so that by the time he got up and hobbled about the hotel on his cane, her glance had become a caress. But each night, in the privacy of her own room, she would remind herself that Mart Joliffe had driven her father's sheep off the rim, had driven her father to suicide. She would nurture her hate with memory, and renew it, so that it never died but instead became a growing cancer in her thoughts. And each day she became a more convincing actress.

She began to notice that Mart watched her more and more. The brooding — so nearly continuous in him immediately following his return to consciousness — bothered him less and less. He smiled oftener and, occasionally, would laugh outright.

One afternoon in mid-December Lucille answered a knock on her door to find Howie Frye standing there, hat in hand, a diffident smile upon his sallow, seamed face. She was startled.

He said, "Missus, could I talk to you for a minute?"

She did not know the reason for Howie's visit, nor the nature of whatever it was he had to say. She did know, however, that his visit might give her an opportunity to probe his hatred of Mart, and for this she wished complete privacy.

So she said, "Why, I guess you can. Will you come in?"

"Thanks."

He stepped into the room, and she closed the door behind him.

"Won't you sit down?"

"Thanks." He perched on the edge of a straight-backed chair and laid his hat on the floor at his feet.

"What did you want to see me about?"

"You were with my girl some the night Joliffe was shot. She left the next mornin'. I found out from the agent at the depot that she bought her a ticket to Denver, but Denver's a sizable place. I ain't heard nothin' from her, an' I was wonderin' if she told you just where she was going to stay or anything."

Lucille gave him a startled stare.

"But she's your own daughter! Didn't she tell you where she was going?"

He ducked his head and stared at his boots.

"No, ma'am. She an' I had a fallin' out durin' the summer over her goin' with Mart Joliffe."

Lucille thought she detected an increased color in his face, a certain guilty overtone in his voice. She asked sympathetically, "Don't you approve of Mister Joliffe?"

She had no information to give Frye, but he did not know that. She intended to pump what she could out of him before she told him she could be of no help.

He looked up at her, his eyes angry, his stare hard. He spoke with emphasis.

"No, ma'am, I don't. Not a little bit."

Lucille's glance was soft and innocent — and sympathetic. "Why?"

The look in his eyes frightened her. She could have sworn that it was jealousy, raw, murderous jealousy. Her surprised mind thought, *But she's his daughter! She's his own daughter!*

His look turned sly. He showed her his yellowed, uneven teeth.

"Lots of people in this town'd like to know that. I jist hate him. I hate him good. I've told him I'd fix him, an' I'll tell you. I'll fix Mart Joliffe good some of these days."

Lucille could not afford now to confide in Frye, nor could she afford to ask his help or even to have it known that she knew him. Yet she felt a stir of excitement that was incomprehensibly mingled with fright. She could be sure of his hatred for Mart. She could be sure of his coöperation in any scheme she might hatch to hurt Mart. The gleam of insane virulence in his eyes assured her of that, even as it frightened her by its ruthless intensity.

His hands trembled, and he clasped them together to still them. He fought himself for control and, when he achieved it, he looked at her. His look had the power to stir terror in her heart, for it was not the look of a man possessed of a whole and healthy mind.

He said harshly: "I just asked you a question, missus, an' you ain't answered it. You know where my girl, Rose, is?"

"What would you do if you found her?"

"Why, I'd bring her back, that's what. I'd bring her back."

"Perhaps she had a reason for not telling you where she was going. Perhaps she didn't want you to know."

Lucille, frightened as she was of Howie, knowing she was treading on dangerous ground, still could not resist the urge to draw him out. His hate puzzled her and, unlike herself, he went to no trouble to conceal it.

He jumped to his feet. His gnarled hands fisted at his sides, dirty, long-nailed. His shirt was stained, black around the collar and sleeves. He needed a shave, and he had a rank, sour odor.

He screeched, "Don't you say that, missus! Don't you say that no more! She's my girl, and I reckon she'll come back if I say so. You tell me, do you know where she is? That's all I came here for. Do you know?"

"I'm afraid I don't, Mister Frye."

Lucille conquered her fear of him, the crawling uneasiness

67

that was sending chill after chill along her spine. She showed him a cold, haughty stare.

"I'm afraid I'll have to ask you to leave. I have done nothing to make you shout at me. There is no reason why I should stand for it."

Now his look turned sly, his voice wheedling. She could see that he did not believe her. He whined, "Now see here, missus, I ain't goin' to hurt Rose when I find her. I reckon you know, but you jist ain't tellin'."

"I'm sorry. I don't know." Lucille's voice was cold, intentionally so. "She left town the day after I arrived. I could hardly have gotten very well acquainted with her. If she would not tell her own father where she had gone, why do you think she might have told me?"

She saw that she had made her denial convincing, but she could see lingering doubts in the man. He stooped and picked up his hat and then, turning it around and around in his hands, he said, "All right. All right. But I'll find her afore I'm finished."

"I'm sure you will, Mister Frye."

Lucille gave him a warm smile. He walked to the door and yanked it open. She could see with what an effort he mastered his frustration.

At last he asked: "Will you let me know if you hear from her? Will you do that?"

"Of course I will, Mister Frye."

He rasped, "Thanks," and closed the door behind him.

For an instant Howie stood in the hallway, his back to Lucille's door. He scowled, and his eyes were deeply puzzled. Lucille Roberts appeared to be just what she professed to be, yet there was that about her which stirred Howie's uneasiness.

He strove to put his finger on this feeling, to pin it down. And failed. Perhaps it was that she seemed too poised and confident. Perhaps it was the fact that he sensed her insincerity. *She knows,* he thought. *She knows where Rose is at.*

He shrugged and went down the hall. On the stairs he passed Mart Joliffe, hobbling upwards with the help of his cane. Mart was terribly thin, a gaunt skeleton of what he had been before Shanks had shot him. His face was drawn and white, showing little trace of its previous healthy tan. Howie could not conceal his triumphant grin. He stopped, for this was the first time he had seen Mart face to face since the night of the shooting.

Mart's first obvious reaction was anger and a desire to go on past without speaking. Yet he did not do this. He stopped, gave Howie a lopsided grin, then said, "Satisfied, Howie?"

For the barest fraction of time, Howie admired him. But then he thought of Rose, and all of the old hatred returned. Howie muttered sourly, "No. You're on the way down, but you ain't at the bottom yet. That's where I want you, and that's where I'll see you before I'm through."

Mart shrugged fatalistically.

"What's eating you, Howie? Rose is gone, so she can't have anything to do with it. Neither Raoul nor myself has ever had any dealings with you."

Howie was silent, thinking his thoughts, letting himself sink into the pool of violence that churned in his brain. His eyes must have reflected his thoughts, for Mart's face quickly sobered. He stared at Howie for a moment more, as though gauging him, evaluating the danger he presented. A new thought brought a flicker to Mart's eyes.

"Howie . . . you didn't hire that gunman, did you?"

In spite of himself Howie started, yet by no sign or change of expression did Mart show that he noticed. Howie grumbled bitterly, "Wish I had. Wish I'd thought of it. By God, you've given me an idea."

He clumped on down the stairs and behind him could hear

the awkward slow tapping of Mart's cane as he ascended. Howie went on out the door and paused for an instant in the street to gather his old sheepskin about him and button the single button that dangled from its greasy front. He reached up and pulled down the ear-flaps on his cap and then turned east off Main towards home.

The sun, sterile and without warmth, laid its slanting rays in the street. The wind, ever cold these days, whipped at Howie and quickly chilled him. Hunched over, miserable, he thought of Rose, then he thought of Lucille. Again he was troubled by the incomprehensible feeling that had stirred in him as he talked to her. He went back, in his mind, over their conversation, recalling it word for word, mumbling it to himself as a dialogue in a play.

He frowned. With his thoughts gradually assuming an orderly form, he recognized that a part of his puzzlement over Lucille was caused by the fact that he sensed an insincerity in her, sensed as well that she had a direct and undeviating mind a good deal like his own.

Her attraction to Mart was obvious to all the people of the town who already were speculating about the date of the wedding. Howie had heard the talk, had thought, *Why shouldn't she be attracted to him? Why shouldn't she want him? He's the richest man in the county.*

But suddenly, following this line of thought, the thing that had bothered him so during and after his talk with her came to him. It had the force of a blow. He mused aloud, "She's been takin' care of him for two months. She'll likely marry him. But she listened to me threaten him and didn't turn a hair!"

Even Howie's hate-twisted mind could recognize the unnaturalness of this. By all of her actions she indicated that she had, if not love, then at least a genuine liking for Mart Joliffe,

70

enough feeling to make the townspeople wink knowingly at each other when the two appeared together in public. Even if there were nothing between them but the natural and necessary tie of nurse and patient, there should still have been enough loyalty in Lucille to make her refuse to listen to Howie's threats.

He kicked this around in his mind for the rest of the distance home, coming to the eventual conclusion as he stepped inside, *There's more to that heifer than meets the eye. She's got her own axe to grind. By golly, I'll bet my neck on it.*

Who, besides himself, could hate the Joliffes, could want revenge against them? Only one person of whom Howie could think. John Robineau. And John Robineau was dead, a suicide months past, the week Mart had brought his steers off the mountain, the week Shanks had arrived on the train with Lucille. . . .

Howie thought, aghast, *Now why didn't I think o' that before?* He murmured her name to himself, "Lucille Roberts," and then "Lucille Robineau." His eyes lighted up and he began to laugh.

The house was cold, and Howie moved around, shivering slightly, and began to build up the fire in the pot-bellied stove that sat in the center of the room. He felt as a man must feel when he is suddenly notified that he has inherited a vast fortune. He chuckled and grinned.

What's her game? he wondered, but he had the answer to that before his question was fully phrased in his mind. *Revenge. She wants to see Mart Joliffe in the gutter, just like I do, and she's willin' to marry him to do it.*

As though reaching a sudden decision, he went to the untidy, roll-top desk and fished a sheet of paper from a cubby-hole. He opened a bottle of ink, dipped a pen in it, and began to write.

Chief of Police.
Denver, Colorado.
Dear Sir:

   In settling the residue of the estate of one John
Robineau, late of your city, we have occasion to dis-
tribute certain personal property and are seeking his
next of kin. Since he was a suicide, we believe you
may have some information concerning the names,
ages, general description, and present whereabouts of
such next of kin. Will appreciate whatever information
you are able to furnish.

                              Howard Frye
                              Cedar City, Colorado.

He did not add, "Attorney at Law." He did not need to.
That would be assumed from the tone of the letter.
   He sealed it, stamped it, and then shrugged again into his
sheepskin coat. Chuckling, he went out the door and into the
blustery, wintry wind.
   As he walked to the post office, his thoughts raced wildly.
For months, in the back of his mind, had slept a plan, a plan
that waited only the appearance of some crack of weakness in
the Joliffe armor. Howie Frye knew how desperately Utah's
sheepmen needed summer grass. He knew that their covetous eyes
were upon Tincup's range. So long as Tincup, personified by
the Joliffes, remained strong and unassailable, the task of per-
suad-ing the sheepmen to move in would be difficult, if not impossible, in view of what had happened to Robineau. But with Mart
Joliffe wounded, a virtual cripple, with a Robineau woman in
the Joliffe household, weakening it with the fungus of her hatred,
betraying Tincup's plans and weaknesses to its enemies. . . .

Damn it, the thing was possible! Howie could enforce her complete coöperation in the very unlikely event that she refused to coöperate simply by threatening exposure.

He slipped the envelope into the slot at the post office, flushed, and felt his excitement rise. On the return walk home, he did not even feel the cold. He was envisioning spring, the relentless tide of sheep moving onto Tincup grass. He was envisioning a tight core of hard-eyed gunmen riding in the vanguard, itching for battle with Tincup's forces. He was envisioning Mart Joliffe, weak from his wounds, embittered and broken by the acid of Lucille Robineau's hatred, too uncaring to put up any real fight. He was watching with satisfaction the inevitable disintegration of Tincup, the eventual utter ruin of the Joliffes. He did not even consider the possibility that he might be wrong about Lucille. Everything he had seen in her, everything he had felt, bore out his conclusion. He couldn't be wrong. He couldn't!

Chapter Eight

The days passed slowly for Mart. He was used to action, to movement, to hard work. He was thoroughly amazed at his own weakness, at his own lack of desire to get back into harness.

He mentioned this to Doc Saunders, and Doc scoffed.

"Hell, what do you expect from a rum-soaked old sawbones? Miracles? You damned near died, boy. You got to give your body a chance to come back." He chuckled. "Marry that pretty nurse of yours. Any fool could see she's in love with you. That'd be my prescription."

He stared hard at Mart with his wise old eyes.

"Think about that. You might find out there's blood runnin' in your veins after all."

Mart did think about it. Lucille was not Rose, but she was a lovely, desirable woman. She had been kind to him, had been completely unselfish all these months, taking care of him. He could never repay what he owed her but, if Doc were right about her wanting him, he could repay a part of what he owed.

A week before Christmas Doc stood up from his examination of Mart and growled, "Go on home, Marty. You'll mend as fast there as you will here. And there ain't a damned thing more I can do for you."

Mart thought of the big house at Tincup, of the comfortable, leather-covered furniture, of hot, crackling fires in the stone fireplace. He thought of the beds at Tincup, soft and warm. He thought of Christmas, of merrymaking and feasting. He did not love Lucille, but Doc had said she loved him. He would make her a good husband, would never let her know that Rose was in his heart, and would always be in it. In time, perhaps, a man could forget. In time, he would grow to love Lucille.

That night as they sat alone in the hotel lobby, watching the dancing play of flame in the fireplace, he said: "A woman and man do not live as close as we have without something growing up between them. Marry me, Lucy. Come home with me to Tincup."

He interpreted the look she gave him, the soft cry she made, as joy.

"Oh, Mart! I've been hoping you'd ask me."

She came to his arms, warm and soft and desirable, and Mart felt a flush of desire. He grinned inwardly, thinking of Doc's words. Then he laughed aloud.

"I'll get a-hold of Floyd. He can go up to the ranch after Raoul and any of the boys that want to come. How about tomorrow, Lucy? Too soon for you? I want us to be back to Tincup for Christmas."

At ten the next morning Raoul Joliffe galloped his hot-blooded bay team into town and behind him rode a score of howling Tincup hands. They swarmed into the white clapboard church at the town's edge, subdued and embarrassed as soon as they crossed its threshold, and Cris Lesback, the town's part-time preacher, intoned the marriage ceremony.

They drove home in Raoul's buckboard with a sour and brooding Floyd Timmons at the reins. For Floyd, perhaps less confused and unhappy than Mart, had recognized Lucille's elation for what it was — triumph. Floyd had sensed, as had Frye, the insincerity of the girl, had known without doubt that her meticulous care of Mart during the long months of his convalescence had been part of her careful planning.

Yet even Floyd's suspicions of the girl could not encompass the full extent of her bitter plans for Mart. Floyd suspected she was merely interested in money and in being Tincup's mistress. He could not know that her interest lay, as did Howie Frye's, in the complete ruin of Martin Joliffe.

Raoul remained in town that first night, getting drunk — celebrating, thought Mart. Yet he was puzzled at the way Raoul had acted after the ceremony. Sour. Sore about something. Grumpy.

Thinks he ought to have been consulted, Mart growled to himself. Yet, if he had stopped to admit it, he would have known this was not Raoul's trouble. Raoul's trouble was the same as Mart's. Raoul had loved Rose, had wanted it to be her Mart married, not Lucille.

Mart jumped down from the buckboard as it whirled into Tincup's yard and drew up before the house. Weakness was momentarily gone in the excitement of the moment. He tossed Lucille up, caught her in his arms while she squealed with pleasure, and carried her up the steps. The massive front door flung open and Fu Ling, the Chinese cook and houseboy, stood framed in it, grinning his wide, toothy grin. His black eyes sparkled with merriment and approval.

"You better, boss. Fu Ling glad. Everything ready. 'Allo, missy. Come in out of cold afore you freeze."

Mart was surprised to realize that Fu Ling was the only one who seemed heartily to approve of this marriage. Smiling down, he carried Lucille into the house, over before the roaring big fireplace where he set her down. But he did not take his arms from around her. He held her quietly for a moment, while his blood began to heat from her nearness, while excitement soared to his brain.

He whispered softly, "Welcome to Tincup, Missus Joliffe."

Her eyes were very soft, and there was a cryptic smile on

her mouth. Fu Ling's slippered steps receded towards the kitchen.

Suddenly, hungrily, Mart's arms tightened. Roughly he drew her close. She raised her mouth to him. He kissed her bruisingly, fiercely, and there was no retreat in her. Fire roared through his body like a holocaust. New strength, new blood pounded through his body. She drew away, her eyes clinging to him.

Her voice was a soft caress. "Oh, darling, do you know how I have dreamed of this moment?"

Behind them, Fu Ling cleared his throat and coughed self-consciously. Mart grinned.

"Fu Ling would like to tell us that there will be time for that later. Meanwhile, he has prepared an excellent dinner for us and has raided Raoul's wine cellar."

"Fine. I'm starved." Her voice was low, filled with tense excitement.

Fu Ling touched a match to the tall candles on the table. Mart held Lucille's chair for her then went around and sat down, facing her. Fu Ling carried in the food. Roast duck, stuffed with apples. Golden baked potatoes. Preserves and delicacies. Steaming, fragrant rolls. Pies and cakes. A dinner only Fu Ling could prepare for this very special occasion.

Afterwards he brought a bottle of Raoul's fine, light wine. And then he noisily left the house, singing. Mart heard the bunkhouse door slam. He looked across the table at Lucille, found her smiling.

He was a lucky man, and Lucille was a wonderful woman. He looked at the years ahead and found them good. There would be children on Tincup, laughing and shrilly yelling in the yard. Blood began to pound hard in Mart's veins. He rose, carried his glass in to the sofa before the fire. Lucille curled up in the opposite corner.

Mart laughed at himself. There had been a time when he

could drink straight whiskey all night and still handle himself. Not tonight. Sickness had done its damage. He was feeling even these few glasses of wine, feeling them in a heady sense of well-being.

He whispered, "Lucille, you're beautiful. I love you. I'll always love you."

Her smile as he said "I love you" was triumphant. The fire flamed and died, and the coals dwindled to a pile of gray ashes. Talk with Lucille was good, but so was silence. At last she rose, timid, conscious of his eyes upon her. She waited while he rose to his feet.

Gently, as though lifting a child, he took her into his arms, lifted and carried her up the wide stairway.

For the first time in weeks Mart was up early. There was a goodness to the morning, and the sun was bright. He dressed and went downstairs. He went out onto the porch and stood looking at Tincup by sunrise, and he felt a new life coursing through his body.

He walked around the yard, inspecting everything, though it was all as familiar to him as the palm of his own hand. He went back into the house to make coffee and had a fire going by the time Lucille came downstairs.

He smiled at her.

"Good morning."

He was puzzled by the look she gave him. There was no softness in it, no warmth, no love.

He said: "What's the matter?"

For answer she laughed harshly. Mart crossed the room and put his arms about her. But she was stiff, resisting.

"Let me go."

"Not until you tell me what's the matter."

Suddenly startling him, she fought free. Her nails were like claws, raking the sides of his face. He stepped back, appalled. Her laughter had died, and now he heard her voice, unbelievably hard, the bitter, vicious voice of a harridan.

She said in a cold, controlled bitterness: "You fool! You stupid fool! Don't you know who I am? Don't you know who you've married?"

So hideously startling had been this sudden change in her that Mart, chilled and horrified, simply stared at her uncomprehendingly.

"Lucille Roberts?" She laughed again, harshly, a bit wildly. "That was my mother's maiden name. I'm Lucille Robineau . . . do you hear? . . . and I'm your wife!"

Mart stood for an instant unbelieving, utterly shocked. Then he caught her arms, and his fingers were like claws. She did not struggle. She simply stood and withered him with her hate-filled eyes. Mart flung her from him in disgust.

His action was reflex, like that of a man whose hand has closed upon something and suddenly realizes that it has touched a snake. Shock gave way slowly to anger in Mart, and the anger gave way to puzzlement.

He asked: "Why did you marry me then? What do you want?"

He could see the thoughts that flickered within the darkness of her eyes. Defiance — and hate, consuming, corrosive hatred that turned the beauty of her face to ugliness. Mart didn't really need an answer to his question. The fact that she had married him was enough. She wanted revenge. She wanted to see him unhappy. Well, she should have been pleased enough all winter. She had seen in him the pain of his wounds, the emaciation they had caused in his normally healthy body. She had seen in him the bitterness Rose's desertion had caused. She had seen him brood and scowl. She had hardly seen him smile. Then she had given his life back to him by marrying him only to snatch it away again, only another torture

79

for one already tortured.

He repeated dazedly, "What do you want?"

She smiled at him mockingly.

"I'm Lucille Robineau. That ought to be answer enough." Her eyes flamed emerald green now. "Do you know what my father did after you slaughtered his sheep? He killed himself. He put a gun into his mouth and pulled the trigger."

Mart had not known. He seldom bothered to read newspapers, never read them at all in summer when the work was so heavy. He'd had no time to read them in Cedar City the night he was shot. And if Raoul or Floyd had read of it, they had not told him. Her words came as an almost physical blow to him.

He muttered, "No, I didn't know."

"He didn't really kill himself. You killed him!"

Mart said resignedly, softly, "I suppose it's no good trying to explain it to you. You have lived with your hate too long. Your father brought his sheep onto Tincup grass after I had warned him not to. I warned him repeatedly after that first time . . . four more times, to be exact. I told him that we couldn't allow him to stay. It was not that your father's sheep were hurting us particularly. We could have stood that all right. But Utah is full of sheep, and they're all short on summer grass. If I had allowed your father to stay, there would have been thirty thousand sheep on Tincup's range within a month, and Tincup would have been out of business."

"So you butchered them. You ran them off the rim. You broke my father's spirit, and he killed himself."

Mart saw no point in telling her that driving the sheep off the rim had been Raoul's idea, had in fact been Raoul's orders. He would not now shift blame to Raoul's shoulders. It had been Mart, himself, who had carried out the orders.

Listlessly he repeated his question, "What do you want?"

His patient tone seemed to infuriate her. She whirled on him, tiny, filled with ugly hatred. He was watching her face, totally amazed at the realization that this was the same girl he had married not twenty-four hours past. Her tone was sharp, clipped, decisive.

"Money, to begin with! Lots of money! Murdered sheep come high."

Mart said: "All right. Then what?"

Lucille laughed scornfully.

"Don't think you're going to get off that easy! I'm your wife. I'll stay your wife. I'll live here at Tincup. And when you die, I'll be there by your side, laughing. Do you hear? Taunting you!" Her laughter grew bitter — and wild. It grew to hysteria, and she made no attempt to halt it.

Mart looked at her a moment more, his face twisting. Then he slammed out of the house.

Dazedly he walked across the yard. He walked across Tincup's broad fields, and beyond them, all the way to the cedar-clad hills. He walked until he was exhausted and only then turned his steps back towards Tincup.

But there was no joy in going back as there had been yesterday. Because now Tincup meant only misery. And there seemed to be nothing at all he could do to change it.

Chapter Nine

Christmas passed, its merriment strained, and the New Year came and went. January wind whistled and sighed against the stout house at Tincup. It snowed, and it cleared and snowed again. In February the wind came, piling drifts to the eaves, clogging the roads, making even feeding the cattle a nightmare of icy, chilling work.

In the bunkhouse, Tincup's crew sat before the pot-bellied stove and played poker, pitch, and solitaire, or they sprawled on their bunks and speculated about what went on between Mart Joliffe and his wife up at the big house. Raoul Joliffe lost weight, turned haggard, and his pithy humor disappeared. His eyes sank deeper into his head. The corners of his mouth turned downward and stayed that way. Mart gained no weight, no strength. Only Lucille Joliffe seemed happy, and even her happiness had a brooding, unhealthy aspect about it.

March came, bringing a howling, zero wind out of the north. For days it beat against the house, until it seemed that its force would beat out the windows, would tear off the roof, would collapse the walls.

Mart watched Lucille surreptitiously and, finally during mid-March, sure at last of the thing he suspected, he went one night to her room. She sat before the huge mirror that had been his mother's brushing that red hair, brushing with steady, even strokes. She counted the strokes, he knew. A hundred in the morning, a hundred at night.

Her skin was flawless, white as milk. The eyes she turned towards him flickered green.

"Don't come bursting in here without knocking, Mart."

"Be damned to that. You're my wife."

His tone failed utterly to conceal the repugnance he felt for her. Her eyes turned greener. The hazel was gone entirely from them now. She wore a thin, gauzy nightgown, as transparent almost as glass, but the sight of her beautifully shaped body stirred no feeling at all in Mart. He was watching her face, marveling at the transformation that hate could cause.

She stood up, faced him and, in a gesture he knew to be automatic, ran a slim hand over her abdomen, absently smoothing. Mart's eyes turned cold. This completed her hold over him.

He said: "You're pregnant."

She stared at him for a moment and then came a cold smile that scarcely touched the edges of her thin lips.

She said softly: "You know, then? You know that I am carrying your child."

She controlled herself with an effort and, when she spoke again, it was calmly, yet she could not keep a note of triumph out of her voice.

"You know this is what I've prayed for. Now I have really got you where I want you, Martin Joliffe. Do you realize how many accidents can happen to a baby? Do you know how many of them smother in their cribs?"

The veins in Mart's temples throbbed, yet his face turned white. Thin he was and weak, but there was no weakness in the hands that clutched her shoulders and bit deep, deeper, until she cried out with pain and struggled to be free.

He said harshly: "You won't do that."

He stared at her hard. He was thinking how easily he could break her tiny body, how terribly easy it would be for him. Lucille took a backward step, her eyes widening.

Mart growled again, "You won't do that, and do you know

why you won't? Because . . . for one reason . . . if you do, I'll kill you . . . with my hands. And I'll give you another reason why you won't. Money. I'll give you thirty thousand dollars the day you turn him over to me, sound and healthy. If anything happens to him, I'll chase you across the world until I find you. And when I do. . . ."

His great hands clenched and unclenched. He began to tremble with the effort he made to suppress his rage. Finally he said: "Pack your things. Tomorrow morning you're going to Cedar City. Raoul owns a couple of houses there. Take your pick of them and stay until the baby's born. I'll pay your bills at the store and give you a couple of hundred a month for yourself. But I don't want to see you again until the baby is born, do you hear?"

Lucille opened her mouth to speak, but Mart interrupted her.

"Thirty thousand is a lot of money, a lot of money to pay for revenge. Thirty thousand and your life is too big a price. And I promise you, Lucille, that's the price you'll pay. If anything happens to that child, that's the price you'll pay."

His rage had turned icy, and it chilled her. For once she was silent. Mart turned his back and went out of the room, slamming the door behind.

Lucille turned again toward the mirror, seated herself once more, and resumed combing her red hair which was losing some of its luster. Mart could not know what passion she had felt toward him that first night, after their wedding. He had put her down at the door of the room that had been Raoul's and his mother's so long ago.

"The lamps are lighted," he had told her. "The room is ready for us. Go on in. I'll come later."

He had opened the door for her and she could feel his eyes watching her as she had moved into the delicately furnished, softly lighted room. Then he had gone down the hall to his own room.

Half an hour later, obviously filled with a bridegroom's nervous apprehension, he had entered the bridal chamber. Lucille had blown out all the lamps. A crescent moon, setting in the west, had laid its cold glow across the bed, lighting Lucille's beautiful body. Trembling, Mart had settled himself beside her.

With a little cry she had flung herself against him, demanding, urgent. At that moment he had been all she had dreamed a man could be. He had been life. He had been love. She had been fragile and delicate, and he had been earthy and strong. Between them had burned the fire that burns the dross from the body and replaces it with newer, stronger tissue. Time had seemed endless, nonexistent in their sharp, sweet ecstasy.

No, she had only meant to torment Mart. She would never end the life that was within her now, even though she might never permit him to see, much less to know, the child they had conceived in that night of passion.

The automatic strokes of her hand holding the hair brush stopped. She was staring at herself in the mirror, and the tears were streaming down her cheeks. Not even the night her father died had Lucille felt such abject, total, and consuming despair.

The face he had showed her had been brutally, coldly sure, but the face he wore as he stepped back into his own room was full of quiet terror and uncertainty. Indecision tortured him and he whispered to himself, *Did I do right? Does she think more of money than she does of the child? Does she think I could kill her? Or will she kill the child?*

These were questions that had no immediate answers. Yet to have showed her any sign of weakness would have, he knew, doomed the child instantly. This way, at least, he had a chance.

He stripped off his clothes and stood looking at himself in

the mirror on the massive oak dresser. He was skinny yet, almost emaciated. Muscle and bone were all he had left. There was no flesh on his body. His skin was white, and on one side was the ragged, red scar where Shanks's bullet had entered, another further back and larger, where it had come out. On his leg the scars were larger — Doc's knife scars where he had cut the bullet out, the cross marks of stitches.

Mart raised the leg, flexed it. It was stiff, stiff and sore. He walked with a noticeable limp and, when he was tired, the pain spread from the wound up and down his leg until it permeated his whole body, robbed his brain almost of other consciousness.

Doc had said the leg would heal. He had promised that it would be as good as new. Yet it did not seem to be healing.

Mart crawled into bed and blew out the lamp. Perhaps sending Lucille to town was a mistake. People would talk, would inevitably discover the reason she was there, would discover her true identity. But until they did, Mart would lose their respect. He shrugged fatalistically. He admitted that anything was preferable to living in the same house with her, reminded every time he saw her, every time he heard her step, of who she was, why she was here.

Too, he felt he owed it to Raoul to get her away from Tincup. He had not missed the loss of weight from Raoul's lanky frame nor the dourness that had lately come over his father. He had not missed the way Raoul picked at his food, and he had heard Raoul pacing the floor of his room in the small hours of the morning.

He stared tonight with mounting horror at his life, lying in wreckage, in ruins. Rose Frye, the only woman he could ever love, was gone. The bribe he promised Lucille would bring Tincup to the verge of bankruptcy. Mart himself felt only half a man. . . .

Yet within all the Joliffes ran a streak of stubbornness, a streak of cold, raw courage. Mart, lying still in bed, clenched and unclenched his fists, and his anger began to grow. It was not sudden, spectacular anger. It was slow-growing, steady anger that would mount and mount with the months until it either broke the binding chain of circumstances that shackled Mart or destroyed him.

At seven the next morning Mart heaved Lucille's trunk into the back of the Tincup buckboard. He stood motionless while she laid her smaller alligator bag beside it and then climbed to the seat unassisted. There were no good byes, only cold, unfriendly stares between the two. Floyd Timmons, scowling, took up the reins and slapped the backs of the team.

Since Floyd was foreman, it was hardly his job to drive the buckboard. Yet Floyd was Tincup, as much a fixture on Tincup as the great old house. Tincup's troubles were Floyd's troubles, the Joliffes' responsibility, Floyd's. Mart wanted Lucille delivered safely to Cedar City, settled in one of Raoul's houses. Floyd would see that Mart's wishes were accomplished.

Great clouds of steam rolled from the horses' nostrils. As they stepped away on the packed and frozen snow, their hoofs and the wheels of the buckboard squeaked against its smooth, frosty surface.

There was little need for words between Mart and his wife. They appeared to understand each other perfectly. What remained between them now was as cold as the still, sub-zero air this morning, sterile as the frozen ground underfoot. Mart shrugged as the buckboard whirled out of the gate onto the road and then turned back toward the house.

He was sweating from the exertion of carrying out Lucille's heavy trunk. He could feel himself shaking, perhaps partly from the cold but partly from weakness. As he opened the great, wide door the friendly heat of the roaring fireplace struck him, and he saw Raoul, tall, white-haired, standing before it, waiting.

Raoul's hands were held behind him, fingers spread to catch the heat of the fire. They were thin, bony, blue-veined. Mart was struck, suddenly, unpleasantly, with the way Raoul had aged in the past three months. He made himself grin. He had hoped to get Lucille away before Raoul was up. Raoul had taken lately to lying in bed until about seven-thirty. This morning he must have sensed something amiss and arisen early.

Mart said lamely, "She's going to stay in town for a while. Says it's too cold up here."

Never yet had the trouble between Mart and Lucille been discussed between them. Raoul had respected the reticence of his son. Mart, himself, had not wished to burden Raoul with any additional worry concerning Lucille's desire for vengeance and Lucille, probably realizing that Raoul's action, if he knew, would be direct and sudden, had refrained from telling him anything and probably wouldn't until such time as he would be powerless to intervene and when the blow would have its most telling effect. Now Raoul's eyes were frosty beneath his bushy white brows.

"Don't lie to me, son. You quarreled with her. A long time ago. The first night you brought her home."

Never in his life had Mart been able to deceive Raoul. He nodded reluctantly.

"What about? There's more to this than one quarrel. People make up, unless it's something they can't make up. She's got her room, and you got yours. That ain't no way for a man and wife to live."

From Raoul that was an accusation, an accusation in this case tempered with tolerance only because Mart had been hurt and was still weak. Raoul waited for an explanation, but Mart remained silent. Raoul was old, weaker than he himself would admit. Mart saw no reason for burdening him further. Yet would it not be better for Raoul to get it now, here, than to wait until some later date and get it cruelly, tauntingly from strangers?

Raoul himself did not seem inclined to let it go this way. He muttered, "I've been quiet about it all winter. But when a Joliffe sends his wife away from him, then it's not a thing to be kept secret forever. You tell me, boy, or by Jupiter I'll saddle up and ride to town. I'll get it from you right here, or I'll get it from her in town. Take your pick, boy."

Mart peered at him in the flickering light from the crackling fire, in the cold, dim light that filtered through the window. He knew that determined look in Raoul's pale, old eyes. He knew that set in Raoul's jaw. He shrugged.

"I was only trying to spare you."

He hesitated, trying to think how he could put this so that it would be less of a shock to his father.

Finally he said: "It all seemed innocent enough when it started. Lucille came to Cedar City the night I was shot. . . ."

Raoul interrupted, "You ain't trying to tell me she had any connection with that killer?"

"No, I don't think that. But I'd been after Rose that day to marry me. I'd thought all along that it was kind of settled. I even counted on it. When Rose turned me down, it came as a terrible shock."

"She say why she turned you down?"

"She seemed scared of something. I wouldn't let it drop, and finally she said she had another man. But I knew she was lying about that. She was scared and, come to think of it, it wasn't for herself she was afraid. It must have been for me."

"Mebbe she knew that killer was comin'. Mebbe she knew you was goin' to get it."

"No. Rose would have warned me. Raoul, I'm damned sure that the killer surprised her as much as he did me. It was

Rose who yelled out her window and saved my life. When I came to a week later, she was gone."

"I talked to her the mornin' she pulled out," Raoul said. "I was pretty rough on her. She stood an' took it like a lady, but it didn't stop her from leavin'." His high forehead creased with puzzlement, but then he seemed to return to his original question. "What's all this got to do with Lucille?"

"I don't know. But I've got a feeling that whatever is happening is all tied up together. Lucille made herself pleasant. She nursed me and took care of me. Maybe she knew how men are with their nurses. Anyway, I asked her to marry me, and she accepted."

Mart grinned with the pain of memory. But he kept on grimly.

"The next morning was awful. . . ." He paused and then repeated: "It was awful . . . that coldness, that mockery in my ears. She was suddenly savage . . . clawed at me, 'til I thought she'd gone plumb crazy. Finally she told me who she is."

Raoul asked, patiently, sarcastically, "Who is she?"

"Robineau's daughter. Now, you damned old fool, do you see what's been happening? Do you see why I've been sleeping in another room?"

Raoul sat down on the sagging leather sofa. He leaned forward and stared into the flames. His face was gray, colorless. When he spoke, it was as though he spoke to something in the fire.

"She hates us, then, and married you to get even." He looked up at Mart. "There's more you ain't told me. Why'd you send her to town?"

Mart sat down beside him and buried his face in his hands. Suddenly it felt good to have someone to share this with, even though he knew the burden was too heavy for Raoul.

"Because I was afraid I'd. . . ." He rubbed his forehead and, although it was cold, it was beaded with sweat. "She's going to have a baby, and she has threatened to kill it."

He saw the anger come to Raoul's face, the wildness, then he saw it leave, and Raoul sank back helplessly. He asked lifelessly, "What you goin' to do?"

"What can I do? I sent her off to town to live. I told her I'd pay her bills until the baby was born and then afterwards, when she brought it to me, I'd give her thirty thousand dollars."

Raoul had gone white, and his gnarled old hands shook as they rested upon his bony knees. Mart stared at him.

"I told her that if she hurt the child, I'd break her in two . . . that I'd kill her with my own hands."

Raoul released a long, pent-up sigh. "She believe you?"

"I think so. But I couldn't do it. No matter what she did, I don't think I could touch her." He fished a sack of tobacco from his shirt pocket and began to shape a smoke. "I'm sorry, Raoul. Your whole life has gone into Tincup. Now I've let a woman wreck it. But I had to make it big enough so that she couldn't turn it down. I couldn't let her do what she threatened to do."

Raoul was utterly silent.

Mart repeated, "Raoul, I'm sorry."

"Sorry? Why, you damned young pup, Tincup is yours anyway. You think I'll live forever? I ain't worried about Tincup."

But he aged years in the next few moments, and Mart was shocked at the aging process. Finally, Raoul stood up. He gripped his son by the elbow and steered him towards the kitchen. He even managed a sour smile.

"I been wondering why you didn't get well. Now I know. Come on. Let's eat."

The anger that had been born last night in Martin Joliffe began to grow anew. But it was helpless anger — terrible, helpless anger. There was nothing he could do — nothing. Lucille had laid her plans too well, and luck had been on her side, the luck that made her pregnant and hardened her iron grip on her husband. There was nothing he could do now. But later. . . . He scowled.

"Raoul, I'm going to work this morning. It's time I started getting well."

Chapter Ten

Above Tincup the valley narrowed, slowly, imperceptibly, and the walls of the mesa on either side rose ever steeper, providing shelter from the howling winds of winter, providing too a well which caught the daytime sunlight and stored its heat against the bitter night. This was Tincup's winter range, where the snow thawed days after it fell, where the grass was long and dry. It was Tincup's winter range, but it was not enough. So the weak and the old were brought regularly to the ranch in winter and fed from the rich, green haystacks there. When spring came, a third of the herd would be clustered about the fenced stackyards, and the other two-thirds, above in the valley, would have stripped the ground bare of feed.

Mart started out riding. A crew of three rode the upper valley every day, and Mart rode with them. It was not a hard task nor an exacting one. They rode, and they talked. They spent the day in the saddle. Perhaps all night they would drive slowly before them a half dozen they had culled out during the day. Perhaps they would drive none. But it was a winter job, and winter jobs are scarce in cattle country. Most ranches laid off their extra hands after the final roundup. Tincup never did. And Tincup earned the loyalty of the crew by this simple gesture.

The first day exhausted Mart utterly, but he stayed with it. He came in that night, spent, beaten, his face twisted from the cruel pain of his leg wound. The second day he was up as usual at daylight, and at sunup rode out again. If it were possible, the second day was worse than the first. The second day he did not even eat but clumped up the stairs and fell onto his bed fully dressed.

Raoul watched him silently. He did not urge him to quit nor to take the easier course — breaking himself in gently. Raoul knew that in bodily punishment lay a cure of the ills of the mind. Mart was taking this cure, a far better one than the one Raoul had once employed, that of drowning all thought in liquor.

Raoul, himself, one day saddled one of the bays and rode into Cedar City. He was weary by the time he reached the town. Weary and filled with the melancholia of age. But, determinedly, he dismounted before Doc Saunders's door and clumped through the snow to the porch. Doc seldom used the front door. The stable, where he kept his horse and buggy, was out back. Only scattered callers ever used Doc's front door.

Doc was a bachelor, and his house looked it. Once a week a town woman came in to clean, but between times the litter collected, and Doc simply kicked it aside and ignored it. Today Raoul was lucky. Doc answered the door, only a little surprise showing in his face.

"Well, sakes alive! Howdy, Raoul. How's Mart gettin' along?"

"Fine. He's working. How's his wife?"

"Comin' along fine. You gettin' anxious?"

"Anxious for you to know what you're up against."

He sat down on Doc's sofa after first pushing aside an accumulation of old papers, Doc's clothes, and Doc's bag. Then he briefed Doc quickly and brutally on the happenings at Tincup, on the identity of Mart's wife, on her intentions towards her baby.

"I want you to watch that girl. I want you to be prepared to tell me, if anything happens, whether or not she had anything to do with it."

"That's a hard thing to ask a man to do. And it won't stand

94

up in court. If she's what you say she is, there won't be a damned thing you can prove."

"All right, but I want to know anyway. I ain't thinking of taking her to court."

Raoul rose, turned, and stalked to the door. Doc stood watching him reflectively as he swung stiffly to his saddle. Raoul put spurs to the hot blood, and his long, lanky body whipped back in the saddle as the startled horse leaped. He took the icy turn and headed towards Tincup at a hard gallop, the hoofs of his horse scattering gobs of snow and mud behind.

Howie Frye, whose eyes missed nothing, saw Raoul ride out from his vantage point on the hotel verandah. Howie had, a couple of months before, received a reply from Denver confirming his suspicion that Lucille was Robineau's daughter. He had kept his silence, feeling that to reveal Lucille's identity would be to forewarn Mart as to whatever her plans might be. Now, however, since it was obvious that Mart knew she was a Robineau, it occurred to Howie that he could drum up a pretty good case against the Joliffes in Cedar City if the town knew who Lucille was.

The Joliffes stood high in the community. Yet always there is an element in any town that, while benefiting from the business of the big ranches, nevertheless feels a certain disgruntled envy and is always ready to seize upon a story that will bring discredit to their owners.

Howie stood up, stretched, and headed for the saloon. Mid-March had brought a respite to the storm country, and the sun beat down warmly on Main Street. A Chinook was blowing in from the south, thawing the snow, turning the street into a sea of mud. Howie could hear the ice in the Little Snake cracking and grinding, as the pressure of water broke it up and started it moving.

He toed open the saloon door and shuffled across the sawdust floor to the bar.

Pete Stoddard grunted: "What'll it be, Howie?"

Howie jerked a thumb towards a bottle half way down the bar, and Pete slid it to him along with a glass. "Swede" Johanson, the barber shop proprietor, stood five feet away from him on his left, and Joe Herdic perhaps ten feet on his right. Howie poured his drink and downed it.

"Kinda feel sorry fer that little woman of Mart's," he said.

Herdic eyed him suspiciously.

Pete Stoddard grunted: "Why? Looks to me like she's doing all right."

"Guess she is if bein' run off is doin' all right."

Stoddard placed both hands on the bar before Howie. He said unpleasantly: "You sure you know what you're talkin' about?"

Howie felt like grinning, but he did not. He mustered an angry expression.

"You're damned right I do. It's a shame, that's what it is. Just because she's a Robineau, he booted her out. Mart hates sheep. He hates sheepmen. He hates a sheepman's daughter, even if she happens to be his wife."

He had the full interest of everyone in the saloon now. Herdic said unbelievingly: "You mean to stand there and tell us that Mart's wife is Robineau's daughter?"

"That's what I said, ain't it? I said it was a damned shame, too. She came in here last fall, an' all she wanted was to try an' make Mart pay fer them sheep. Her daddy shot himself over in Denver and didn't leave her a dime. But before she had a chance to say anything about it, Mart got shot."

Howie liked to be the center of attention. He liked this feeling of all eyes being upon him.

He went on, "She didn't have no money. Mart needed someone

to look after him, so she took the job."

Herdic scowled. "Looks to me like she'd have hated Mart."

"Sure. She should have. But she didn't. Look at the way she took care of him. Doc says she was as good a nurse as he ever seen. There ain't no figgerin' women. She was around Mart all day, every day, an' she fell in love with him. He asked her to marry him, an' she took him up on it. But I reckon she was scairt to tell him who she was. She knew how he hated Robineau. She knew how he hated sheep. So she kept quiet, an' used her mother's maiden name when she got married."

Herdic whistled. "Well, I'll be damned."

But Pete Stoddard would not give up. He would not accept this damnation of Mart from Howie Frye's lips. He said: "I don't believe it."

Howie shrugged. "Hell, I don't care whether you believe it or not. Looks to me like the facts speak for themselves. Some way or another Mart found out who she was. Mebbe she let it slip. Anyhow, did it make any difference to Mart that she was expectin'? Hell, no! He booted her out, sent her to town. An' I'll tell you somethin' else. You know what's goin' to happen when she has the baby? Mart's goin' to take it an' run her clear off." He shrugged eloquently, spread his hands before him. "Hell, mebbe he'll give her a couple of thousand dollars to get rid of her. But he'll do it. Wait an' see."

He had not gone this far before, even in his thoughts. He did not know that Mart intended to run Lucille off, but it seemed the logical thing for Mart to do. He would not continue to live with a woman who hated him as Lucille did. He couldn't.

Pete Stoddard grumbled, "I don't believe it. Mart ain't that kind."

Howie only shrugged. Pete would come around. He poured himself another drink, fully aware of the dead silence in the saloon, the silence that was as condemning of Mart as would have been a flood of angry words. The people of Cedar City, like people in all small cow towns, were a warmly sympathetic bunch, particularly towards women. Howie could feel sure that his story would be common knowledge in town by nightfall, and would be embellished and enlarged until every woman in Cedar City would be highly indignant. Tomorrow Lucille would have callers — dozens of them.

Therefore, if he wanted to see Lucille himself, he had better do it today. He tossed off his drink and rang a quarter on the bar. Pete Stoddard frowned at him helplessly, and Howie grinned maliciously. He went outside, pausing a moment to roll a cigarette, hold it to his thin lips, and light it.

Then he put his head down and scurried across Main and up the side street that led to Lucille Joliffe's house. As he walked, he considered with satisfaction what he already had accomplished. He had sown the seeds that would completely discredit the Joliffes in a matter of days. Now he had only to lay the groundwork for the complete defeat of the Joliffes this coming spring. The Joliffes could do a lot of things that ordinary people couldn't, so long as they had the solid good will of the community. But with the people against them?

Howie grinned. With the people against them, the Joliffes would also find that the sheriff was against them. The Joliffes were a power in the community, but they did not elect the sheriff. The people did that.

Howie knocked sharply on Lucille's door and, after a few moments, she answered it, gazing at him suspiciously. He was amazed at the change the months had wrought in her. She was thinner. Her face had grown older and showed an unwonted sharpness, almost a harshness. Hate, he thought, had wrought these changes in her, even as it had made the perpetual sourness in Howie Frye. How could he know it was misery?

She asked sharply: "What do you want?"

Howie grinned ingratiatingly. "I want to help you, missus, if you'll ask me in. You remember, I hate Mart Joliffe, too."

"Why?"

"It's a long story, but I ain't a-goin' to tell it to you standin' here on the porch."

"How can you help me?"

Frye's face grew hard. His eyes glittered. He shrugged and started to turn away. He muttered, "I thought you hated him. I thought mebbe you'd like to see him fixed. I guess I was wrong. Good bye, missus."

"Wait!" Her hesitation finally vanished. "Come in."

Howie Frye grinned his sour grin, but there was triumph in his narrow-set eyes. He was like a turkey buzzard alighting on carrion, savoring, relishing, full of ghoulish anticipation. He stepped into the dim and dingy parlor, which was neat enough, and sat down on the sofa.

Lucille took a straight-backed chair across from him. She said irritably: "I don't know why I let you in. I'm doing all right without you. Mart Joliffe has been desperately unhappy since the day I met him, since the night that man shot him in the street."

Howie grinned.

"You owe me something for that. You might never have married Mart if he hadn't been shot."

He leered at her.

"I put that gunman on Mart, only I told him to shatter Mart's knees so's he'd never walk again."

His face twisted.

"The fool bungled it."

Lucille's eyes widened.

Howie said: "I've helped you other ways, too."

He told her the story he had just related down at Stoddard's.

She began to smile, but it was a cold and humorless smile.

She asked: "How can you help me?"

"We can help each other. We can wreck Tincup for him. There's half a hundred sheepmen in Utah that are itchin' to move in on Tincup grass. All they need is a little encouragement. All they need is someone to organize them so they'll move all at once. And they need half a dozen gunslingers to head them up and give them courage. I can do the organizing. I can hire the gunslingers. You can furnish the money to hire them."

Her eyes had turned suspicious at the mention of money, but he gave her no time to consider her reservations farther.

"I've turned the town against him today. The sheriff does what the townspeople tell him to. Mart won't get away with the things this spring that he did last spring. If he kills anybody, he'll hang. If he destroys any sheep, he'll go to jail. And if he don't fight, he'll lose Tincup."

Still Lucille showed hesitation.

Frye cackled. "By golly, when it's all over, you can let him know that it was his own money that whipped him."

That turned the tide.

Lucille asked: "How much do you need?"

"Mebbe a thousand to begin with. Another thousand later. I don't know. Gunslingers come high."

Lucille stared at him, but he could see her mind churning, could see wicked pleasure growing behind her eyes. She stood up finally and went into the kitchen. She came back in a moment, carrying a glass fruit jar that contained a jumble of gold and silver coins, a wad of paper bills. She dumped it out on the table.

"He gives me two hundred a month and pays my bills at the store. But most of this I got from him while I was living up there."

She counted the money rapidly, then said, "There is almost eight hundred here. Is that enough?"

"I'll make it do."

Howie could hardly keep the elation out of his voice. He could make the sheepmen themselves put up enough money for the hire of the gunmen. This eight hundred was Howie's own, to pay his expenses while he traveled around in Utah.

"How do I know I can trust you?"

He shrugged and looked at her with his cold, expressionless eyes.

"You don't, but you'll take the chance. It's an eight-hundred-dollar gamble for you, and you don't really give a damn about the money. You want what I want, and that's to see Mart Joliffe in the gutter, broken, beaten, and crippled. Maybe even dead."

He stood up.

"Make up your mind. If I'm going to do this, I've got to get started. The sheepmen will want to move by the first of May."

"All right." She shrugged almost imperceptibly. She shoved the pile of money at him. "Take it."

Frye stuffed it into his pockets. He was grinning.

"You won't regret it, missus."

He picked up his hat and sidled to the door. He heard the wail of the train as it sat in the station awaiting the time of departure and, as soon as he was again in the street, he started to run. When the train pulled away from the station, he was on it, looking back at the squat and ugly shapes of Cedar City, smiling his evil, triumphant smile.

Lucille watched Frye's figure retreating down the street, through the mud and slush. Why had she done it? Why had she given him what money she could spare? For once she knew the answer with certainty. Her loneliness, her misery at the predicament in which she now found herself had become intolerable. If Frye could finish the Joliffes, that would be an end to it. They would most probably be too involved with the invading sheepmen to think much about her and the baby. As soon as she could, she and her baby would disappear, just as Rose Frye had.

Chapter Eleven

Howie Frye, hunched and morose, sat in the worn velour seat of the train coach heading westward into Utah and stared out at the flat desert landscape. He thought of Mart Joliffe. He thought of Rose. He thought of the years that were gone and wondered at length what changes he could have made in the way he'd lived them, changes that might have altered the way things had ended.

His hatred for Mart went back a long way. Contrary to Mart's belief, his hatred was born of jealousy, pure and simple, the kind of jealousy that had rankled and grown until it had consumed his entire life. Rose had been but a small child when Howie Frye came to Cedar City, newly married to her quiet, sweet-faced mother. She was not really his daughter, but he had seen no reason then to make the fact known. That was his first mistake. If Rose had but known all along, things might conceivably have been different.

Seven or eight years later her mother had sickened and died, and Howie had been left alone with the girl, then twelve. He could remember Rose growing up, growing lovelier every day. He could recall the way his own interest in her had increased after she had begun to fill out and look like a woman. Howie had been a lonely man, one to whom women did not take readily. He had been long without a woman, and Rose was really not his own daughter. So, he told himself emphatically, there was nothing really wrong in his attraction to her.

Yet, because of the people of Cedar City who did not know that he was not her father, he controlled his feeling towards

Rose, even managed to hide it for a time. He watched her grow. He watched her grow so breathtakingly beautiful that it wrenched a man's heart just to see her coming up the walk from school.

He listened to her confidences, listened as she bared her young love for Mart Joliffe, and it was then that the seed of hatred was planted in his heart. Hatred born of enraged futility because his hands were tied, because he was old, and she was young, because he could never have her so long as she thought of him as her father, so long as Mart unwittingly held her love and her loyalty.

Mart Joliffe was young — young and heedless — not even noticing Rose because she was a couple of years younger than he. Lord! Howie would have traded the world to be but two years older than Rose, five years, even ten. He lived with this for five long years. Alternately, he hated Rose and loved her. He hated himself for the feelings he could not control. Often as not he was surly towards her, cross and angry without justification save that overpowering, denied hunger.

She was bitterly unhappy during those years — terribly in love with Mart, crushed because the only interest he showed her was the polite, passing interest he showed to all the town's girls younger than himself. And Rose's unhappiness only served to increase Howie's hatred of Mart until it became an obsession with him, greater even than his love for Rose. These two rankling things he had lived with for five long years. An unrequited, hopeless love and a hatred that festered and grew. Both things became more intense because of the fact that Howie must daily live in Rose's presence. He was so near her when she dressed, changed clothes, when she took a bath in the large copper tub.

A dozen times he swore to himself that he would go away or that he would send her away, but he had not the strength to do it. He could not bear to deprive himself of her, of the exquisite torture of her nearness.

Things had drifted on. Howie traded in livestock, horses, land, town lots, anything that could earn him a dollar, as he had always done. Rose had seemed uninterested in men at all, but Howie had noticed that her face would light up wonderfully whenever Mart Joliffe came near. Mart must have seen it at last. He must have seen the fire that burned in Rose for him, for he took to seeing her, taking her to the town's dances at the Odd Fellows Hall on Saturday nights.

Perhaps it was her association with Mart that brought it on. At last there came a time, as Howie had known it inevitably would, when he lost his stern control, when he took Rose hungrily and clumsily into his arms and told her he was not her father. He had groped her hard young breasts and caressed the curve of her voluptuous hip. Lord, how he had wanted her!

Even now, more than a year later, his face would color and grow hot as he remembered her biting scorn, her utter terror. Since for this he dared not hate Rose, so he hated Mart Joliffe the more.

Rose moved to the hotel after that and lived on the small legacy her mother had left her which Howie had preserved more or less intact. Howie had seen her less. Mart had seen her more. In late summer, last year, maddened by the knowledge that she would marry Mart when he returned from roundup, he went to her one night, told her plainly that, if she married Mart, he would kill him. He knew she had believed him. He knew as well that he had severed finally the last tie that bound Rose to him. Knowing this, in utter bitterness, he had sent to Denver for Shanks.

Now Rose was gone, gone out of his life forever. Only Mart Joliffe remained, and Howie Frye's hatred of Mart remained.

The train puffed westward, and night came down over the broad, flat desert. Tomorrow, at last, Howie's hatred could translate itself into action, and he could begin to build the chain of circumstances that would utterly destroy the Joliffes.

Snow was almost gone from the desert. It lay yet, dirty and gray, in the shady draws, but in the open the ground with its sparse cover of grass was bare, sere and brown for as far as the eye could see. In the far distance, to the east, Howie could make out the high, rocky escarpment of the Tincup Plateau, a thin, indistinct line along the horizon. Sun beat down into the single street of the town of Tillman as Howie stepped onto the sagging hotel verandah.

The entire town was no more than a quarter-mile long. At one end of it was the tiny railroad station, across from this the livery stable, gray and weather blasted from the nearly continuous desert wind. Huddled against the stable was a saloon, closed and locked at this hour of the morning, and a vacant lot's width from the saloon was a tiny restaurant before which a couple of horses drowsed, hip-shot, soaking in the warmth of the early morning sun.

The hotel before which Howie stood was a two-story affair, sadly in need of paint, which looked as though it might collapse, and whose sign bore the unimaginative and obvious legend:

Tillman Hotel

A bare town. A drab town. Howie swung his glance up the street with complete disinterest. His eyes touched the windmill, slowly turning in the exact center of the one street, feeding a tank which squatted in a foot-deep wallow of mud. Beyond the windmill were the town's business establishments — a general store, a hardware store, and, surprisingly, a dressmaker's shop.

106

A band of loose horses strayed through the residential district at the town's upper end and gathered about the water tank in the center of town to drink, laying their ears back at each other, biting and kicking, crowding for a place at the tank.

Howie shrugged, stepped down off the verandah, and walked towards the restaurant. Its window was dirty, almost opaque with grease and fly specks. At the counter sat two men, apparently the owners of the horses out front. Howie took a seat one stool removed from them.

A Chinaman, his face shining with sweat, shuffled in from the kitchen.

Howie said: "A couple of eggs and bacon. Some coffee while I'm waitin'."

He stirred cream into the coffee and studied the man nearest him at the counter. He judged the man was about thirty.

He asked: "This is sheep country, ain't it? Who's the biggest sheepman hereabouts?"

"Huh? Oh, I'm damn' near a stranger myself. But I can tell you that. It's Anthony Poulos. Why? You huntin' a job?"

Howie found his appraisal of the man bogging down. He looked like neither cowman nor sheepman, yet there was the stamp of the outdoors on his darkly tanned face, in the fine lines that framed his eyes, eyes that were ice-green and utterly without warmth of expression. Howie felt a quickening of his interest and dropped his glance to the man's side, saw then what the eyes had told him would be there, a low-swung, cleanly oiled, holstered Colt .45.

Howie grinned inwardly. "No, but I might be hirin'. Hirin' guns."

"For what?"

The man showed no open interest, but Howie could see that he felt it.

Howie said: "Sheep an' cattle ruckus."

107

The Chinaman brought Howie's eggs. Howie directed his attention to his food now, ignoring the man beside him, but he could feel the man's eyes upon him, studying him. From the corner of his eye he saw the other one lean forward and stare at him. The second wore a beard, black and ragged, but his eyes had the same cold stamp that characterized the first.

The bearded one asked: "What you payin'?"

Howie shrugged. "Depends on who I hire."

"You a cattleman?"

Howie shook his head but did not explain. He finished his eggs in silence and wiped his mouth with the back of his hand. Winter was long and jobs scarce. He would have bet a hundred dollars that these two did not have more than a couple of dollars between them. But they looked like what Howie wanted.

He gulped the last of his coffee and fished a sack of tobacco from his pocket. He knew it would help his argument when he faced Poulos if he had a couple of hardcases like these two with him. He had made his bid. Now it was up to them.

He touched a match to the end of his cigarette, inhaled deeply, and stood up. He fished the tight roll of bills Lucille had given him from his pocket and peeled off one, which he laid on the counter. The Chinaman made change

The first one, the smooth-shaven one, said: "I'd like to hear more about what you got in mind. Hank and me ain't busy just now."

Smiling at the Chinaman, Howie sat down again and pocketed his change. The Chinaman inquired if Howie wanted more coffee. He shook his head, no. As soon as the Chinaman retreated back into the kitchen, Howie turned on his stool to face the two hardcases at the counter.

"Sheep are goin' to move in on Tincup over in Colorado this spring. Tincup ain't going to like it. I want maybe a dozen men that can make Tincup take it anyway. Tincup is tough.

The men I hire have got to be tougher."

The man grinned mirthlessly. His teeth were even, white. His face was thin lipped, flat planed, bony. His nose was long and sharp. He shoved his battered Stetson back to reveal reddish, thinning hair, and stuck out a hand.

"My name's Ben Corbin. This here's Hank Moya."

He grinned suddenly, showing Howie the faintest bit of warmth.

"Mister, we been broke so long we ain't even going to ask you which side is the right side in this ruckus you're talkin' about. But when we fight, we aim to get fightin' wages."

Howie took the outstretched hand.

"You'll get 'em. I'm Frye. Howie Frye. You want to take a ride? We'll talk about it, an' you can show me where Poulos's place is."

Corbin shrugged and looked at Moya. Moya nodded slightly, his eyes hooded and blank. Corbin made a thin-lipped grin.

"All right. Let's go."

Now, at seven-thirty, a few solitary souls had begun stirring about in the streets of Tillman. A graying, stooped man who looked like he had neither washed nor combed his hair since rolling out of bed swung open the wide, squeaking doors of the livery barn and went in. Howie turned around and headed that way. Behind him, Corbin and Moya untied their mounts and swung easily to their saddles.

They waited outside while he hired a horse, and the old man saddled him up. Then Howie mounted, and the three rode out of town, crossing the tracks and taking the north road.

Silence, the utter silence of the desert, lay over the land. In a few moments the town was behind them. Howie dropped to the rear of the column, and instinctively his hand went to his inside coat pocket where a tiny Colt .41 rested. Treacherous himself, Howie expected no less than treachery from those with whom he dealt.

The miles dropped behind. Once, Corbin's horse halted at an arroyo for a drink and, when he started up, he was behind Howie. Howie turned, his eyes cold.

"Move ahead. You're broke. I ain't. And I don't know you yet. But I'll tell you one thing. You try for me, and you'll not only miss out on my money. You'll miss out on wakin' up alive tomorrow mornin'."

He lifted out the Derringer and fondled it lightly in his hand. Corbin laughed.

"Reckon I might have been thinkin' about it. But you'll do. You can quit worryin' now."

Howie thrust the gun back into his pocket.

"I wasn't worryin'. You was doin' that."

He knew then, very suddenly, that the next three months would be the most dangerous of his life. But he recognized as well that the first few days of organization would be the worst. After that he would have the weight of the sheepmen behind him.

At eleven they sighted a string of low buildings ahead, and Corbin swung around in his saddle.

"Anthony Poulos's outfit. He runs damned near ten thousand sheep."

Howie grunted. He was studying the layout as they drew nearer. Plainly, Poulos was almost as big a man as Mart Joliffe. As they rode into the bare yard, Howie spoke to Corbin.

"Hang back. I want to talk to Poulos alone."

A man came out onto the wide verandah of the house, a thick-set, grizzled, dark-skinned man. He looked questioningly at Howie and did not miss Corbin and Moya, nor did he miss the efficient guns they carried.

Howie asked: "You Anthony Poulos?"

Poulos nodded.

Howie asked: "Lookin' for summer range?"

Interest flickered in Poulos's eyes. He nodded guardedly. Howie jerked a thumb towards the east.

"Plenty over there . . . if you know how to get it."

Poulos shook his head.

"Robineau tried that. He didn't do so good." He spoke with a heavy accent.

"The Joliffes are done. Feller shot Mart Joliffe last fall, and he ain't recovered from it. Robineau's girl rigged him into marryin' her, an' you can imagine what she's doin' to him. The old man's aged ten years this winter. You been wantin' Tincup's grass. You'll nèver see a better time to take it than this spring."

"Where do you come in?"

Howie laughed. "I knew you'd ask me that. I want to see the Joliffes broke and beaten. I want to see Tincup split up and sold off in little chunks."

The old intensity of hatred was in his voice and in his eyes.

"You want more than that."

Howie nodded. "Five thousand for myself after Tincup's grass is yours. Wages for half a dozen gunslingers while we're taking it. Your backing and the backing of all the others you take in with you."

"That all?"

Poulos's dark eyes were sardonic. Howie felt a stir of anger.

"No, by God. I want to run the show. I want Mart Joliffe to know when it's over that I did it to him."

"How do you plan to do it?"

"Easy enough. I know Mart Joliffe, which is something you don't. Mart's got a soft streak in him. He feels guilty about Robineau's sheep. The woman will be workin' on him."

He swung down from his horse because he could talk better with his two feet on the ground.

"Move up in small bunches but all at once. Scatter 'em all over Tincup grass. Make him think each outfit is separate. He'll hesitate long enough for you to get all the sheep you want to on Tincup grass. By the time he sees you're organized, it'll be too damned late."

Poulos drew a cigar from a vest pocket and bit off its end. He said: "He'll fight then."

"Yeah, maybe, but his heart won't be in it. He's paid too much for that Robineau deal."

Howie jerked his head at the two hardcases, Corbin and Moya.

"I'll hire half a dozen more like them. We'll bring Mart Joliffe to his knees, and you'll have Tincup's grass."

Poulos, stocky, squat, puffed furiously at his cigar for a moment. Finally he spoke.

"I ain't going to say yes or no to a proposition like that on the spur of the moment. You give me a week to think it over. I got to see some of the other boys."

Howie's face hardened. He said sarcastically, "You hand a man a fistful of gold, and he don't want to take it. He thinks there's something wrong. If you don't want this deal, there's plenty of others that do. You're the biggest one around here, but you ain't the only one."

Poulos's eyes turned hard.

Howie said: "Two days. It's damn' near the first of April now. If you're goin' to do this, somebody's got to get a move on. I can't pick up gunslingers just anywhere. It all takes time."

He stared at Poulos, his eyes slitted and angry. Finally Anthony Poulos shrugged.

"I need the grass. I been figurin' I'd have to sell some sheep. With Tincup grass, I could buy more." He made a cold smile. "Two days. I'll drive around and see the others today and tomorrow. Come back tomorrow night."

Howie shook his head. He knew when he had won. He said: "No, you drive into Tillman. I'll be at the hotel."

He wheeled his horse and at a gallop went out of the yard, his two hired guns falling in naturally behind him.

Chapter Twelve

Rose Frye usually rose at six-thirty. From habit she washed and dressed at once then built up the fire in the tiny stove in her living quarters behind the dressmaking shop. She prepared her own breakfast. Usually she had two cups of coffee, and this morning was no exception. Afterwards, she went into the shop and began her day by sweeping the floor and dusting.

Often she would pause and stand before the window to stare out across the barren desert floor eastward towards the visible thin line that marked Tincup boundaries. For so many weeks she had stared at that same landscape each morning so that she could do so now without feeling the pangs she had known at first, without having her eyes mist over with tears, without feeling her crushing loneliness and isolation.

The Tillman Hotel was on the same side of the street as the dressmaker's shop, so she did not see Howie Frye until he crossed towards Lin Chang's restaurant. Even then she could hardly believe her eyes. How could Howie have found her here? He thought she had gone to Denver.

And she had, but she had not stayed. The big city was too much for her. She missed the open vastness of the range country. She missed the feeling it gave her that Mart was not entirely lost to her.

There was really no excuse for a dressmaking shop in Tillman. Tillman was too small a town. Rose scarcely made her groceries out of it even though she was good and got all the business there was to be had. While she still had a good part of her mother's legacy, the dressmaking shop had reduced somewhat

114

the drain on it besides keeping her busy, keeping her from thinking too much about anything.

She began to tremble as she watched Howie's scrawny figure cross toward the restaurant. Lin Chang was a kind and gentle man. He would not betray her. Yet, she could not tear herself away from the window after Howie went in and so, later, when she saw him come out, she perceived that he was now on apparently friendly terms with those two strangers who had been in Tillman less than two weeks themselves.

Rose immediately thought with quiet terror, *He knows that I am here. What does he want? Why won't he leave me alone?*

It puzzled her when Howie headed down street towards the livery stable, when he mounted, and with his two companions took the north road out of town. *Perhaps he is not after me,* she thought, *or he would have come here directly. Then what was in Howie's devious, unhealthy mind? Not an innocent, aimless ride on the desert. Howie hated riding, hated horses. No, whatever brought Howie to Tillman was important but, if it was not concerned with herself, then what could it be?*

Rose shook her head. She went about her work, preoccupied, troubled. She hung the capacious folds of Mrs. Poulos's dress from the dummy and knelt beside it, her mouth crammed with pins, but she could not keep her mind on the dress. Time after time she wandered to the window and stared out into the street. The town was filling with men from the outlying ranches, and at last Rose was forced to stay away from the window altogether.

She did not dislike the dozens of men who paid her such persistent court. She was even a little flattered. There were three or four she liked who would, she knew, have been glad to have her on any terms. They had said as much. But Rose was too honest to give the man she married such a small part of her as she had to give. Most of her — all of her heart —

belonged to Mart Joliffe and perhaps would always belong to him.

So, whenever possible, Rose avoided her suitors and today stayed back from the window whenever one passed. She had not yet relinquished all hope. Some day, something might happen to Howie, or he might go away. Then, if Mart still wanted her, she would return to him.

Mrs. Poulos was to have been in this afternoon for a fitting, but she did not come. Watching for Mrs. Poulos, at two o'clock Rose saw Howie ride back into town, saw him stable his horse, and walk toward the hotel. She studied the two he was with as they left him and headed into the saloon.

Even to Rose the way their guns hung advertised their calling. Saddletramps. Drifters. Gunmen, men who hired their murderous talents and who were always to be found in a country where trouble was shaping up. *What did Howie want of them? Was he planning more trouble for Tincup?*

With a sigh of relief Rose saw Howie turn out of sight into the hotel with never a glance upstreet towards the dressmaking shop. He was not after her, then, perhaps was not even aware that she was in Tillman. And, indeed, how could he hurt her if he did know? She was of age, dependent only upon herself. Howie was not even her father.

Mrs. Poulos still did not come in, even though Rose lingered in the shop all afternoon waiting for her. Instead of having dinner at Lin Chang's, as was often her custom, she ate her late meal in solitary, brooding silence and then went to bed early. For endless hours she lay awake, worrying about Howie, about his errand in Tillman, and a dark suspicion began to form in her mind.

Tillman was at the heart of eastern Utah's sheep country, lying close to the edge of Tincup's domain. Conceivably, Howie was trying to stir up the sheepmen, trying to persuade them to take over Tincup's range as soon as the grass turned green.

Eventually, though she despaired of so doing, she dropped off to sleep only to dream of Mart, standing with his back to a wall, with Howie and his two Tillman acquaintances closing in on him from three sides. In the dream Howie's face was a mask of snarling rage, and the other two were coldly sure. Rose screamed, "Mart! Look out!" and woke up.

She was on her feet beside the bed, shivering, and she realized with wonderful relief that her cry had been the only real part of the dream. She was perspiring, but she was also cold. She got up and made herself a cup of tea, sat sipping its scalding warmth gratefully. But the hideous reality of the dream would not fade from her mind. She thought, *Mart is in danger . . . in terrible danger.* Desperately she wondered what she could do to help, and finally, finding no ready answer to this, crawled back into bed, and in the small hours of morning slept.

On the following afternoon, late, Mrs. Poulos drove into town with her husband and came at once to Rose's tiny shop, her broad face smiling apologetically.

"That Tony! I plan to come in yesterday as I told you I would, but no! These men, they have always got something else to do."

Rose smiled wanly.

"That's all right, Missus Poulos. It didn't matter."

Mrs. Poulos put a thick arm around Rose and squeezed her affectionately.

"You are a sweet girl. It was not Tony's fault, I think. Some stranger come out yesterday morning . . . something about grass . . . and then Tony had to hitch up the buckboard and go see his neighbors about it. Today, Tony has to come to Tillman to see this stranger. . . . again. Don't you feel well, Rose?"

117

"I'm all right, Missus Poulos. I didn't sleep very well last night."

Rose helped her slip into the unfinished dress, frowning worriedly. She knelt, tugging at the dress, and spoke finally around the pins in her mouth.

"There are several strangers in Tillman. What did he look like?"

Mrs. Poulos laughed, made a mock shiver.

"I did not like him. He was small and skinny, like an elderly bantam rooster. He had two others with him."

Rose's heart sank. She did not feel that she should exhibit more curiosity, yet she felt that she had to be sure. When she saw Howie step across the street towards the saloon, accompanied by Poulos, she was sure enough in her own mind, and yet the question came from her lips.

"Is that the one?"

Mrs. Poulos nodded violently. "That's the one." She seemed to lose interest in Howie. "When will the dress be ready? Could you have it by Saturday?"

"I'll try, Missus Poulos. I'll surely try."

Rose had to force her smile as the woman left. Then she sat down and buried her face in her hands. First Shanks. Now this. Howie would, she realized at last, never be satisfied until Mart were dead, perhaps would not be satisfied even then. It made no difference apparently to Howie that Rose had given up Mart. Rose thought with desperation, *Oh, I've been such a fool! Why didn't I tell Mart? Why didn't I tell the sheriff? Why didn't I stay?*

Suddenly, determinedly, she stood up. *I can tell him now. I can go back and tell him now.*

She did not know that Mart had married Lucille. In her excitement at the thought of going back, Lucille did not even occur to her. And perhaps it was just as well, for if she had

118

known, she might not have caught the night train for Cedar City.

Anthony Poulos sat across the table from Howie Frye and poured himself a drink.

He said: "We think we will go along with you. But one thing we do not like. You say Mart Joliffe has a soft streak. Perhaps this is so. You should know Mart better than I. But I know old Raoul. There is no soft streak in Raoul."

Howie laughed unpleasantly.

"Hell, he's an old man. Mart runs Tincup, Mart and Floyd Timmons, an' Floyd does what Mart says."

Poulos shrugged.

"Perhaps. But I know Raoul from the old days, and a man does not change. Raoul is hard as nails. There is no weakness or pity in Raoul. There is no regret in Raoul over Robineau's sheep."

"Damn it, he's an old man. He can hardly get around."

Poulos shrugged expressively.

"He can speak, can he not? He can give orders? And he can plan a fight?"

"Well, I guess he could. But like I told you. . . ."

Poulos's expression was stubborn.

"I have put my life into my sheep. My friends . . . the ones who wish to go with me in this . . . have done the same. We will take a chance, but we will not be fools. Get rid of Raoul, or we make no deal."

Howie stared at him. He saw the implacability of final decision in the old sheepman. He asked viciously, tauntingly: "You mean . . . kill him?"

Poulos smiled.

"I did not say that. The methods you use are your own. I am only interested in results. Get rid of him."

119

"That'll cost money."

Poulos shrugged. He fished a small leather bag from his pocket. "I have some money here."

He flopped it onto the table, and it struck a blow like a sledge against the table top.

"There is a thousand dollars here. There will be more when you need it."

Howie studied the old man's broad face. It showed him ruggedness, imperturbability, the firmness of decision. The man, Howie knew, was like all these big ranchers. To them, the ranch was all important, and the methods they used in building it were not particularly important. He felt a touch of contempt. In their minds they could justify anything, even murder. Yet in Poulos's own way, he was scrupulously honest. He had a certain code, and he lived by it.

He was not Howie's sort of man, but suddenly Howie knew that there would be no quibbling from Poulos in the weeks to come about how he handled the invasion. Poulos had chosen his course, and he would travel it to the bitter end, no matter who got hurt, no matter what the cost. He grinned.

"Get your sheep ready and stop worrying about Raoul. I'll take care of him."

Poulos stood up but did not offer his hand, an omission Howie did not fail to notice. Poulos said: "I'll be ready to move the last week of April. But I want to know about Raoul before I move. I want to know that Raoul will not be planning Tincup's defense."

It had just occurred to Howie that this was one way of striking at Mart that had not previously occurred to him. He grinned viciously. What other blow could he strike Mart short of killing him which would cause him so much pain?

He said shortly, "You go ahead. Raoul will be dead in three days."

Later, Howie sat at the same table and stared across it at the flat, expressionless eyes of Corbin.

"I've got work for you. Your regular pay is a hundred a month, for each of you. There's a two hundred and fifty dollar bonus for this particular job, and you split that. All right?"

"What's the job?" Moya asked.

Howie noticed Moya, really noticed him suddenly for the first time. There was an odd sort of excitement in the man's eyes, a wildness Howie had not noticed before. Beneath the black beard the man's lip twitched. Howie glanced around the saloon and lowered his voice.

"A killing."

Something flared like a grass fire in Moya's eyes. He grinned and licked his lips. Howie noticed that Corbin's expression as he looked at Moya mirrored much the same thing Howie himself was feeling.

Corbin jerked his head at Moya. "He's your man," he muttered disgustedly. "Hard times and an empty belly make a man run with some queer ones. He likes killin'."

Howie felt cold. He said: "We all go together. I point him out, and the two of you take care of him. When we get back, I want you to take a ride down into Arizona. I want eight or ten more men, men that can shoot and ain't afraid to. I'll give you money enough for expenses and fifty dollars apiece for each one you bring back."

"When do we leave?" This was Moya, but his eyes were hooded and showed Howie no emotion.

"Tonight. Go on down to the stable and hire me a saddle horse. Hire a pack horse too. I'll go down to the store and buy some provisions, and I'll meet you there." He hesitated a minute, and then rose. "We'll go into Tincup by the back door. That way, when the job's done, there'll be no one to

121

know who did it."

He watched them file out the saloon door. A buckboard passed at that moment, and the thin, distant wail of a locomotive whistled across the desert. A woman sat in the buckboard beside the driver and for an instant, in the brief glimpse he caught of her, a sense of familiarity was strong in Howie. But the anticipation of this new blow he was about to strike Mart was too great in him for further consideration of the woman. Just someone he had seen in Tillman, he surmised, and promptly forgot her.

He did not forget Mart, nor did he cease to think of what he would do to Mart. He began to grin and this way went out of the saloon and moved uptown towards the general store.

Chapter Thirteen

Spring always came with a rush to this high storm country. Mart felt the soft breeze blowing out of the south and reined in his horse, just to smell the goodness of it, the fragrance of thawing, fertile earth soaking in sunshine so very hungrily. Willows along the creek bank were a brilliant red-brown as the sap rose in them and budded with velvet gray pussy willows. A light patina of green lay over the fields, spring green, and cattle roamed the valley, gaunt from winter but bright eyed with hope of a new, lush year.

He gazed across the yard at the sun-washed porch, at Raoul sitting there in his creaking rocker. Raoul was thinner than he had been last spring. Mart thought back over the past year, realizing how many things had happened, how many unpleasant things. Robineau had tried his grab for Tincup graze and had killed himself because he failed. Rose had run away. Mart had been shot. He had married Lucille Robineau.

On those cold damp spring mornings, Mart could still feel the stiffness and pain in his leg, the sharp bite of agony as he drew frosty breath into his lungs. But he had stopped limping, mostly by vowing fiercely to himself that he would not limp. He had gained weight. He felt better, almost as well as he had felt before being shot. Almost as well in his body but not in his mind.

The guilt over Robineau's sheep had been washed away largely by Lucille and by the bitter things she had done to him. Now, considering it carefully, he realized that he did not hate Lucille, perhaps he would never hate her, not even if she carried out her dreadful threat. A deep sorrow was what he felt for her. She had thoroughly ruined her own life. Women were so much more vulnerable than men, Mart guessed. They should never try to fight men on a man's terms. They only got hurt. Mart himself would recover much more quickly from Lucille than Lucille would from Mart, and even this would be cause for more bitterness. It would hurt her to realize that, in exacting vengeance from Mart, she had hurt herself more deeply than she had hurt him.

Shrugging lightly, he crossed the yard and swung down before the corral. He unbuckled the cinch and slung the saddle to the top corral pole. He turned the horse into the corral, hung his bridle from the saddle horn, and then hung the blanket beside the saddle to dry.

Avoiding the deeper mud in the yard, he crossed and clumped up the steps to the porch. Raoul gave him an idle smile. Mart squatted, removed his spurs, and fashioned a cigarette.

He said: "Took a ride up on top this morning. Grass is coming. Another two weeks. . . ." Some prompting in the back of his mind reminded him of what he had seen on the plateau. He mused aloud. "Funny thing, though. I cut the trail of three riders an' a pack mule. Who in the hell would be up there this time of year?"

Raoul shrugged. Mart felt saddened at the lack of fire in Raoul's eyes. He had done that to his father. He had done it by letting Rose go, by marrying Lucille.

Raoul asked: "When you going to put cattle up there?"

"I thought I'd put Floyd to gathering some of the younger steers next week. They'll make out all right up there, even if there ain't much feed. Calf branding will take a couple of weeks more, and we'll push them all up."

He watched Raoul as he spoke. He was thinking, *Hell, I've never seen him before when a warm spring wind wouldn't heat his blood. Usually he's in the saddle from the first thaw on.*

He said, on sudden impulse, "It's Saturday. Why the hell don't we saddle up and go to town? We'll get drunk together like we used to do."

Raoul showed him the frosty blue of his fierce old eyes, the ghost of a smile on his grayish lips.

"What would your mother say?"

It was an old jest between them. Mart played his part seriously.

"I'm a man, damn it. I can drink by myself, so why can't I drink with you?"

He was pleased to see Raoul's smile widen. Raoul stirred in his chair.

"All right. Saddle me a horse."

Mart stooped to buckle on his spurs. He wondered why he kept thinking of the trail he had cut this morning. It was somewhat unusual for riders to be crossing Tincup Plateau at this time of year, but it had happened before. He thought, *They ought to have come off one of the trails. It would be easier going in the valley.* He straightened.

"You better get your sheepskin. It could get cold."

He went down the steps and across the yard. He hesitated for only an instant over his choice of a horse for Raoul, finally selecting one of the hot-blooded, shining bays. The horse would put Raoul on his mettle, and besides Mart knew the old man would be highly insulted if he were expected to ride a horse gentler than one of the bays. He'd grumble sourly, "Reckon you're an old man for sure when they start saddling gentle old horses for you. Saddle me somethin' that can run, dammit."

Grinning a little, Mart rode to the house, leading the bay for Raoul. Floyd Timmons came out of the bunkhouse. He asked, "How's the grass on top, Mart? Good enough to move cattle up?"

"Not yet. But we'll put some steers up there pretty soon,

next week maybe. Then we can get busy and brand the calves."
He thought again of the trail he had found this morning, and
asked, "You seen any strangers around lately? I cut a trail up
on top of three men and a pack animal that wasn't over a
day and a half old."

Floyd shook his head. Raoul yelled from the porch, and Mart
grinned.

He rode over to the porch and handed Raoul's reins down
to him. Suddenly, so very suddenly he had an odd, gray feeling
of depression. So strong was the feeling, so incomprehensible,
that for a moment he sat utterly still, frowning. It was almost
a premonition, almost a foresight of disaster. It was as though
gray clouds had suddenly drifted in from the north, bringing
cold fog, obscuring the sun.

Yet the sun shone warily through a thin, light overcoat. Floyd,
fists on hips, watched Raoul from the bunkhouse, grinned as
Raoul howled and spurred up the lane. Then Mart's feeling
of depression lessened. There was rich goodness in seeing Raoul
act this way. His father was already half way up the lane.

Mart's legs twitched, and his spurs turned inward towards
the horse's ribs. But he stopped then, reined in the horse that
had already started to move. His rifle nested close to his hand
in the saddle boot, but his hip had not the comforting weight
of his holstered Colt against it. Mart had not worn the thing
for months. Somehow, today, he thought of it again as he had
so long ago, that night in town when he had been shot.

His hunch had paid off then. He could not ignore it today.

Floyd had approached questioningly, and now he murmured,
"Mart, you better take after Raoul. You know how he is on
a fast horse. And the road's still slick."

"Yeah."

But Mart swung down, his indecision gone, and handed the
reins to Floyd. He sprinted for the house, took the steps two

at a time. There seemed to be such an odd sense of urgency in him. He slammed open the door and went directly to the mantel where his gun hung from a set of elk antlers and snatched it down.

Raoul had never had a bad fall from a horse, he told himself fiercely. Why all this damned worry about him? Why this feeling of nakedness without the Colt, when he had ridden without it all winter?

He snatched his reins from Floyd's hand and leaped into the saddle. His spurs raked furrows along the animal's ribs, and the horse plunged away. Behind him, Mart heard Floyd's startled cry.

"What the hell? You see Raoul fall? Why the gun?"

Mart did not answer. He was beginning to feel like a fool. Hell, Raoul was all right. Raoul always rode at a run, in mud, in snow, in deep dust. It made no difference to Raoul what the footing was. He had often said, "The footing's the horse's concern. Not mine."

Almost, Mart slackened his pace, but then the strange feeling of depression returned. Suddenly he remembered the trail of three men and a led mule. He recalled the attack upon him last fall in Cedar City, recalled that Joe Herdic had never succeeded in figuring out a reason for it. Herdic had the firm belief that someone had hired the killer and, if that were so, that someone, whoever he was, could have hired a killer again.

He thundered into the turn where Tincup's lane met the road. His horse floundered in the soft mud, faltered, and almost went to his knees. Automatically, Mart loosened his feet in the stirrups, tensed himself to spring from the saddle as the horse fell. But he recovered and did not fall.

Again Mart's spurs sank deep. The prints of Raoul's horse were deep in the soft mud, and gobs of the sticky stuff lay about on the road where the bay's pounding hoofs had flung them.

Damn the old man anyway! How far would he run? Would he release all of the winter's stored-up energy in these first few minutes? Would he run the bay until the horse could run no more? Mart admitted that it was possible. Raoul had been lately subject to dark and brooding moods. He might be finding release from them in the frantic motion of his spirited horse. And Mart admitted this as well — if Raoul kept his spurs in the bay's ribs, Mart would never catch him, would never see him until Raoul decided to stop. For no horse on Tincup could catch that bay except the other one.

The minutes ran on, and the miles fell behind. Mart's horse dragged his breath with great labored heaves now, and his glossy coat gleamed with sweat and was flecked with foam. And still Raoul's tracks stretched on ahead.

Mart began to curse softly, slowly, steadily. The feeling of depression, of premonition had crystallized now. He knew suddenly that out of today could come nothing good. Some terrible thing must happen today. Someone would die.

He tossed a glance over his shoulder and saw a single rider pounding after him, nearly a mile behind. *Floyd* was the brief thought that flashed across his mind. Then he heard the shot. Flat, wicked, it rolled across the valley and bounced off the high rim on the southern side of it.

Premonition was reality now. Mart scolded himself bitterly, *You're a fool! That trail you cut . . . why didn't you have sense enough to know what it was? Why didn't you ride with Raoul? Why . . . ?*

Seconds were eternities. Mart's cruel spurs drew blood from his horse's sides. He yanked the quirt off the saddle horn and belabored the animal's rump. But he had the horse's whole effort, and the weary animal could give no more.

128

He caught a glimpse of a rider sliding his horse down the steep and muddy slope a half mile ahead. Immediately his view of the man was obscured by a heavy clump of cedars. Mart dragged his rifle from the boot and levered a shell into the chamber.

He came out from behind the cedars, saw the rider dismounting, gun in hand. Even at this distance Mart could see the man's black and bushy beard. He thought, *I'll know that one. I'll know that one.* He flung his rifle to his shoulder, looped his reins around the saddle horn, holding the dangling end with one knee. He steadied his aim as best he could on the running horse and squeezed down on the trigger.

He saw a second man come sliding down the hill out of the cedar jungle that covered it. And he saw a third, sitting his mount on a high point, unmoving, watching. Distance was too great for recognition, but Mart thought with fleeting contempt: *The boss of them. Too good to kill but not too good to hire it done.*

His rifle bucked hard against his shoulder. The bullet kicked up a shower of mud that flung over the bearded man, made him jump back, made him come around, gun held high and ready. Mart fired again, but this one was high and to the right.

Smoke rolled from the man's revolver, and seconds later the report shattered the valley's quiet, flat and wicked but not having the force of power of the first shot Mart had heard.

Mart raised his rifle for a third shot but, as the muzzle came over his horse's head, the animal shied violently, almost unseating his rider, making Mart lower the rifle and grab for the saddle horn.

Mart topped a shallow rise, and suddenly the whole, level expanse of the valley lay before him. He saw the bay, shining with sweat, standing a hundred yards from the still body of

Raoul Joliffe. The horse was trembling so violently that his shaking was visible even at this distance of nearly three hundred yards.

A shout echoed down from the high knoll where the single watcher sat, and both men ahead of Mart swung around to look upwards. Mart could catch no words, but the tone of the voice was frantic and hurried.

The bearded man ignored the shouted command, whatever it was. He turned back towards Raoul Joliffe, stepping carefully, raising his revolver for another shot. Hope coursed through Mart instantly at this, and the racing thought cleared through his mind, *Raoul isn't dead! Raoul isn't dead!*

The other, the one with the bearded man, yanked his horse around and spurred him uphill into the sheltering cedars. Mart's mind instantly warned him, *Remember that man. He's standing in the cedars drawing a bead on you.*

The bearded one shot a glance around at Mart's rapidly approaching figure. He hesitated for the barest instant between his horse and his fallen quarry. Then he turned again towards Raoul, and his gun came up for the second time.

Mart was but a short hundred yards away. His frantic mind shouted, *If you never shot straight before, shoot straight now!* He dropped his rifle and snatched out the Colt .45. Hammer came back in a swift, automatic movement as the gun cleared its holster.

Eighty yards — sixty, fifty-five. The gun bucked against his palm and, almost as an echo, the bearded man fired, not at Mart who thundered down upon him but at Raoul, still and gaunt in the mud, oddly twisted, looking pitiful and small.

Mart's thoughts screamed, *Too late! Too late!*

The bearded man grunted audibly and now swung around, his left hand going automatically to his side, low on his abdomen.

It took the barest part of a second for Mart's brain to register the import of the tiny shower of mud that spattered over Raoul's still face. But then he knew, and fierce gladness surged through him. The bearded killer had missed his carefully placed shot. He had deviated from his aim but a couple of short inches, and it was enough.

In a single swift movement, without checking the animal, Mart flung himself from his horse. He landed, boots digging in, sliding. His gun came away as his arms flung wide for balance. The killer, wicked, yellow fire flaring in his eyes, steadied his own gun on Mart's body.

A rifle roared from the cedars. The bullet struck a rock at the side of the road and whined eerily across the valley. Mart thought — *God! This is it!* — because he could not bring in his outflung arms soon enough, could not gain balance quickly enough to match the bearded killer's deadly speed.

Neither could he stop trying. He teetered there, still in motion, still fighting for balance, and then he saw the glaze begin to cover the killer's evil pair of eyes. It was a dimming of the killing lust, a dying of life's leaping flame. The gun in the killer's hand lowered, and the muzzle dropped. Only then did reflex tighten the killer's trigger finger, and the gun roared, harsh and deafening.

The bullet made a solid, flat sound as it struck the soft mud — like a beaver's tail on the muddy bank of a pond. Powder smoke, acrid and blinding, whirled into Mart's face.

He fell, rolled, brought his gun before him, and trained it upwards towards the green-black cedars. He saw nothing. But he heard the crash of brush as the second ambusher's horse scrambled upwards.

Floyd's horse slid to a stop beside him, showering him with mud. But Floyd did not dismount. Instead, he yanked the animal around and started up through the cedars.

Chapter Fourteen

Mart went at once to Raoul. He knelt in the mud by his father's side.

Floyd stood awkwardly over him, muttering bitter curses under his breath and the almost frantic plea: "Mart, lemme go after them! Don't let 'em get away with this!"

"They won't. They won't."

Mart was almost afraid to touch Raoul. The old man had been knocked from his horse by a bullet, had tumbled onto the muddy road. He probably had some broken bones. And he had that bullet in him.

Apparently, Raoul's head had struck the road first, had plowed a furrow in the mud, for his face was unrecognizable because of the heavy mud coating it carried. Mart stripped the bandanna from his throat and wiped gently at Raoul's face. Blood welled from beneath the mud. Mart spoke sharply over his shoulder.

"We're closer to town than we are to Tincup. Take Raoul's bay and ride to town. Get Doc and a buckboard and come on back. Kill the bay if you have to, but hurry!"

Raoul groaned and stirred ever so slightly. Mart unbuttoned his father's sheepskin, flung it back, and searched with his eyes for the telltale welling of blood that would reveal the wound. He heard the sound of the bay's hoofs on the road.

Afraid to do much to Raoul for fear of aggravating his injuries, Mart nevertheless straightened his legs and arms so as to make him more comfortable. He thought the left leg was broken for it had an odd limpness to it, a limberness that was unnatural.

Blood kept welling through the coating of mud at the side

of Raoul's head, just above the ear. With gentle, careful fingers, Mart probed at this place, smoothing away the mud, until at last he uncovered the wound, a deep furrow that the bullet had plowed. Mart knew that two shots had been fired at Raoul and now knew one had missed.

"Grazed his head," he muttered. "But there'll be concussion . . . maybe a fractured skull."

He closed Raoul's coat and stood up.

If only Raoul were not so old! If only he were not so weak. But in spite of Raoul's age and weakness, hope began to grow in Mart. Raoul had never given up without a fight. He never would.

With the borning of hope, a lot of Mart's grief and shock left him. Anger, slowly growing in him all through the winter, now began to stir anew. He walked to where his rifle lay and picked it up, wiped the receiver with the bandanna, peered into the barrel to see if it was stopped with mud. He walked over and toed the dead form of the killer viciously. He peered up at the screen of cedars, and his mouth made whispered words, *Ride fast and far, boys. Because we'll be coming after you.*

Raoul made a low groan, and Mart's head jerked around. The old man's eyes were open, but they were dull and glazed with pain. His words were weak.

"What the hell happened? That damned bay horse take a fall?"

"You were dry-gulched. Bullet grazed your head. You damned fool, you left me pretty near a mile behind you. It's just lucky. . . ."

Mart's tone was sharp, angry, as his worry found expression in his voice. But he was instantly contrite.

"Sorry. I guess if you hadn't been traveling so fast, they'd have got you dead center."

"You run 'em off?"

"Two of them. The third is still here. He's dead."

"Them was the tracks you saw then?"

"Uh huh. You shut up. Talking isn't good for you. Floyd went after Doc and a buckboard. He ought to be back pretty soon."

He hunkered down on the ground beside Raoul. His hand found the old man's, felt its feeble pressure. Anger grew in him like a flame in a pile of kindling.

He said: "Raoul, I'm getting damned sick and tired of being a duck in somebody's shooting gallery. Last time we had no chance of finding who was behind it because the guy was dead. This time it's different. I'm going to take that trail and stay on it 'til I find them."

Raoul grinned at him wanly.

Mart said: "Herdic won't get them, either. They're mine!"

Raoul grunted. "All right. There's plenty of rope layin' around in the barn. Take some of it with you."

He closed his eyes, smiling faintly. His hand relaxed.

Mart asked anxiously, "Raoul. You all right?"

He heard a distant shout, swiveled his head around, and looked down country. He could see a buckboard rocking along behind a running team. He could see a horseman pounding along beside it. The seat of the buckboard carried two figures, one the unmistakable, short, bulky figure of Doc Saunders, the other slimmer, somewhat taller.

Mart turned back to Raoul. His father's face was ashen beneath its coating of mud. The eyes were closed. Mart slid a hand beneath Raoul's coat, felt his chest where the heart was.

A long sigh ran out of him. The beat of Raoul's heart was weak but steady and unfaltering. *Passed out,* thought Mart. He got up and walked to his horse. The animal was soaked, chilled, and shivering. There would be no trailing until fresh horses could be caught, and that meant a trip back to Tincup. The dead man's horse had wandered off, now stood a quarter mile away, head down, giving Mart an accurate estimate of the condition of the ambushers' horses.

He thought, *I could give them half a day and still catch them.*

The buckboard rounded a turn, and suddenly Mart's heart almost stopped. That figure beside Doc, that white, terrified face — the way she sat the buckboard seat, tense, beautiful, wild. Mart's lips formed her name, *Rose!*

Floyd, ahead of the buckboard now, plunged to a halt. He had left the bay in town and was now riding a fresh stable horse. Mart gave him no chance to dismount.

"Get up on the road. Bring a half dozen of the boys and that other bay of Raoul's for us. Make it fast going up but save your horses coming back."

Floyd galloped away, and Mart turned towards the buckboard. Doc was climbing clumsily and stiffly down, but Rose had dropped the reins, had flung herself to the ground beside Raoul. She had no thought for the inch-deep mud she knelt in. Her head went down, and her soft, fragrant cheek laid itself against Raoul's. Her midnight hair cascaded around his head. Her shoulders shook with her sobbing.

Doc said gruffly, "Get her up. How the hell is a man supposed to get a look at Raoul?" But his voice was hoarse.

Mart caught Rose beneath her arms, stood her up, turned her around. Her eyes were wide, frightened. He had the feeling that, if he released her, she would run.

Mart said gently, "Raoul's leg is broken. He's got a bullet burn on the side of his head. But he was awake a minute ago. I talked to him. He'll be all right."

There was mud on Rose's face — mud and Raoul's blood. She asked, her face utterly without color, "Do you know who did this?"

Mart gestured with his head at the dead gunman on his back in the mud, staring sightlessly at the sky. Rose looked at the man and shuddered.

"Howie did it, Mart. Howie did it. Two days ago Howie was with that man in Tillman, Utah."

Mart wondered why he did not feel more surprise. Perhaps he had unconsciously suspected Howie. Perhaps he had known all along but had been unwilling to admit his suspicions even to himself.

Doc stood up, snapped his black bag shut, and wiped his hands on his pants. He observed, "I thought Raoul was a crazy driver. But did you ever ride with Rose?"

Rose asked: "How is he? Will he . . . ?"

"Dunno why the hell he shouldn't. Help me lift him into the buckboard. You diagnosed him as good as I could, Mart. Broken left leg. Concussion from that bullet wound. Barring pneumonia or some damned thing, he'll be up in a week or so."

Mart and Doc lifted Raoul and deposited him on a pile of blankets in the back of the buckboard. Rose covered him tenderly. Doc climbed to the seat and took up the reins.

"I'll drive back."

He clucked to the team, drove ahead. Then he backed, turning the buckboard around in the road.

Mart looked down at Rose. White and still she stood, almost cold. He thought, *She knows about Lucille.*

He asked: "Are you back for good?"

She shook her head and would not meet his eyes.

Conscious that Doc was waiting, that Raoul needed to get into Cedar City at once, Mart nevertheless took a couple of minutes for Rose. He took her shoulders in his hands, waited until her eyes raised to meet him.

He said: "When will you quit running away from me?"

137

"Mart, you're married. I can't. . . ."

He cut her off. "I'm married, but I've not got a wife. We've slept in separate rooms since the night we were married."

"She's carrying your child, Mart."

His tone grew vicious.

"And has threatened to kill it as soon as it's born. Rose, quit it! I don't know why you ran the last time, but I know why you're running now. Give me a little time, Rose. Give me a little time to work things out."

She was hesitating, and he pressed his advantage. Roughly he pulled her to him, crushed his mouth against hers. He wanted to be brutal with her, to force his need upon her, but he found he could not. Tenderness crept into the kiss and, when Mart held her away, her eyes were wet with tears.

He said: "Stay until I can get to town and talk to you. Will you promise me that?"

After a small hesitation she nodded, her misted eyes devouring his face. Then she whirled and swung up to the buckboard seat. Doc clucked to the team and drove slowly and carefully towards town.

When the rig was a hundred feet away, Mart called: "Send Herdic out, Doc."

Doc raised a hand. Rose turned on the seat and watched Mart until the buckboard went out of sight at the bend.

Mart had told her he didn't know why she had run before. Suddenly he did know. He thought he could put it together in his mind. In some way Howie's hatred of him was concerned with Rose. Howie had threatened to kill him in the saloon the night he was shot. He had probably threatened Rose with Mart's death, had told her he would kill Mart if she married him.

So Rose had gone away. *Why didn't she tell me?* Mart wondered, but he had the answer to that readily enough. Howie's threat

138

from her lips would have been nothing new. And you cannot kill a man for a threat. You cannot even jail him. Besides, Rose had undoubtedly realized at what a disadvantage Mart would be against Howie. He could make no hostile move against Rose's father.

Mart was excited at Rose's return, yet he was also vaguely uneasy. Nothing was settled between them. He'd had experience with the implacability of her decisions. But he would at least have another chance at persuading her to stay. She had promised him that.

He walked to the horse he had ridden from Tincup, off-saddled, and then gave the chilled animal a brisk rubdown with the soggy saddle blanket. He took the bridle off and turned the horse loose. It shook vigorously, walked away a few steps, and lay down to roll. Thoroughly muddy but apparently satisfied, it got to its feet and trotted away. Mart caught Floyd's horse, rubbed him down, and turned him loose to trot after the first.

Now Mart turned his attention to the dead gunman's horse. He led it over to the road, dropped the reins and, with some difficulty, hoisted the body to the saddle. With the man's own rope he tied him down and, when that was finished, led the horse up the hill a few feet and tied it to a tree. Herdic would be up after a while and would lead the horse and its gruesome burden back to Cedar City where an attempt would be made at identification and then the body buried.

A high yell lifted distantly to the valley above him, and Floyd came over a slight rise of ground, five men behind him, all trotting briskly. When they rode up, Mart took the bay's reins from Floyd, saddled, and led out along the plain and muddy trail that led upward through the cedars. At the top of the rise, where he had seen the lone horseman sitting, he drew rein and examined the ground for a few moments.

There was evidence here that the ambush had been patient. Cigarette stubs littered the ground. Tracks overlaid one another until nothing was clearly distinguishable. But the running trail of the two leaving was plain enough.

So hurried had been their departure that they had not even bothered with the pack mule, which stood patiently tied to a tree. Beside him were the remains of an old fire and a few cans of beans, unopened. Bedrolls lay on the ground and a blackened coffee pot was overturned near the remains of the fire.

Mart said: "It's Howie Frye and a hired gunman we're after. Kill the gunman if you want, but I've got to have Howie alive."

Howie deserved to die, he knew, but he did not want the man's blood on his hands. Already there were too many barriers between him and Rose. He would not add another.

Floyd rode up beside him at a spot where the ground leveled slightly and cocked an eye at the sky.

"You see what I see, Mart? I think we'd better kick these horses in the ribs a little."

Mart had felt the indefinable change in the air himself. All day a thin film of cloud had lain across the sky. The air was utterly still, and its very stillness was ominous. Mart knew at once what he could expect — one of the sudden blinding snowstorms so common to this high storm country in April. It would whirl and rage for half the night perhaps and would stop in the morning. But it would cover the ground with six inches of white, virgin flakes and, by the time it thawed enough again to pick up the fugitive's trail, it would be useless to follow.

He calculated that they had all of the remaining daylight today and, in a quick decision, came to the hopeful conclusion that, if they pressed their horses, they could come up with their quarry before night and the snow hid their trail.

He touched spurs to the bay's gleaming sides, and the animal surged ahead powerfully. The trail led upward inexorably, and it soon became apparent to Mart that Howie Frye and his companion, also aware of the coming storm, were pressing their mounts to the utmost — a killing pace, a pace that could not long endure — in the hope of staying ahead of pursuit until the snow or the night came down to hide their tracks.

Up across the slide they went, through the rimrock, and out onto the rolling top of the plateau. Now, no longer was it necessary to rest their horses every few hundred yards. It was gallop and walk, trot and gallop — and walk again.

There was little talk among Tincup's grim 'punchers. Floyd had briefed them upon the day's happenings, and they were out to avenge old Raoul.

The hours passed, and the horses sweated and began to lag. And still the trail stretched ahead. A flake of snow struck Mart's face, and at once he realized that the sky was heavy gray, solid. The wind turned colder, and Mart rolled up the collar of his sheepskin.

Floyd rode up beside him, asking, "How fresh do you think these tracks are now?"

Mart grinned at him, a tight grin without mirth. Floyd knew as well, perhaps better than he, how old these tracks were. Floyd could gauge them almost to a minute, particularly in mud that is soft and loses its sharp shapes quickly. But this was a part of Floyd's deference. He never told either Mart or Raoul what he thought. He asked their opinion and then either concurred or gently amended it.

Mart said: "Damned near thirty minutes."

Floyd nodded. "We're licked, then. You know it, and so do I. It's taken us this long to catch up an hour on them. The snow will cover their tracks before we make that other half hour up."

"Unless one of their horses dies. God knows they've been

crowding them hard enough. We might catch them over the next ridge."

Floyd grinned his approval. He grimaced.

"What I was thinking. Their horses warn't in too good a shape to begin with. And they've poured it on today. From the looks of their tracks, they've been pourin' it on harder than we have." He pointed to the ground. "One of them ponies is groggy now."

But the minutes pounded away into hours. The snow thickened, and the creeping gray of dusk rolled over the land. Somewhere ahead rode Howie Frye and his hired killer, perhaps but a mile, a half mile away. Yet at last snow and darkness hid the trail to where not even Floyd could make it out, and Mart reined in with futile anger.

"We could flounder around in the dark all night," he said, "and probably pass them ten feet away and never know it."

He shaped a cigarette and touched a match to its end.

"We'll go back," he murmured softly then, "but we know who we're looking for now. We know it's Howie Frye."

Chapter Fifteen

Floyd wanted to take the boys and get on the train. He wanted to be in Tillman when Howie and his hired killer arrived, but Mart shook his head.

"No. We got the man that shot Raoul. We know that Howie was behind him. We've got nothing particularly against the other man. Let it go. We'll pick Howie up one of these days. Besides that, I want to start gathering steers Monday. By the time they're gathered, the snow will be gone on top. Then we've got to get busy branding."

In early morning he swung down before Joe Herdic's office, more solid and in better physical condition than he had been for months. He could not quite understand the excitement that stirred in him, for none of his problems was solved. He was still married to Lucille and, although Rose was back, he could not see how it could come to anything. Howie was still alive, still wanted him dead — and Howie would try again.

Perhaps his knowledge that spring had come was partly responsible for his lightened spirits. Perhaps it reassured him to have Raoul safely checked in at the hotel, out of danger at least until he could manage to get out of his room.

Joe Herdic took his spurred boots off the desk as Mart came in.

He said: "Tough about Raoul, Mart. You catch the others?"

His eyes were oddly cold as he stared at Mart.

Mart shook his head.

"Trail snowed in. But I know who one of them was, Joe. It was Howie Frye. If he comes back to Cedar City, you throw him in the jug. I'll stand back of the charges."

"You got proof?"

"No." Mart could not understand Herdic's hostile attitude. Neither could he tell Herdic of Rose's accusation. He looked at Herdic hard. "What's eatin' you, Joe? If I wasn't damned sure it was Howie, I wouldn't tell you to jug him. He was back of that gunman that shot me last fall. He was back of this jigger that shot Raoul. Do I have to go get him myself?"

"Better not, Mart. People are getting kind of tired of Tincup's high-handed methods. People are commencin' to think that the Robineau deal last spring was pretty raw but not half as raw as the deal you gave your wife."

Mart could feel his anger rising, could feel the heightened color in his face. Herdic's expression suddenly mirrored outright dislike.

Mart made a wry, tight grin.

"You've changed your tune, Joe. Why? Tincup's never been a grab-all outfit. We've lived and let live, at least in the past ten years. You used to think Tincup was all right, especially around election time. What changed you?"

"Like I said. That Robineau deal. The way you're treatin' your wife. She was willing to let the past die. But not you. You hate sheep and everything connected with sheep, don't you, Mart? Now you hate Howie Frye . . . maybe because you want Rose even if you have got a wife . . . and Howie don't like it."

Herdic had come to his feet as he spoke, stood spraddle-legged and defiant. Mart's big fist smashed his lips against his even, white teeth. Herdic went backward, fell over his swivel chair, and tumbled against a file case. He pushed his hands against the floor and came to his knees. Blood trickled down his chin from his smashed mouth. He turned his head and spat. His eyes were venomous.

Mart's action had been reflex. He stood now in still fury, waiting for Herdic to get up so he could hit him again. Mart's light blue eyes flashed their cold fire.

Mart said softly, too softly, "Joe, if I ever hear Rose's name on your filthy tongue again, I'll finish what I started this morning. I'll ram every damned tooth you've got down your throat."

Herdic's eyes blazed, but he did not get up.

Mart whirled and went to the door. He said intemperately, his hand on the knob, "You remember this, Joe. I gave you a chance to do your job. You wouldn't do it. From here on, I'm taking over. Tincup will handle its own affairs in the future. If you can't do the sheriff's job, by God I'll do it for you."

Herdic crawled to his feet. He fished a clean, white handkerchief from his pocket and wiped his mouth.

He threatened: "Watch your step, Mart. Watch your step. The laws were made for Tincup, same as for everybody else. You break them, and I'll come after you."

Mart felt like laughing, felt like snorting — *the way you're coming after me now?* Yet he knew that would have been unfair. Herdic was something of a dude, but no one had ever questioned his courage, and Mart did not do so now. He knew that Herdic's remark about Rose had been ill considered, that the sheriff was ashamed of it and had not fought back because he was ashamed.

The knowledge did not seem to lessen his anger. He whirled out the door and slammed it behind him. For a moment he fumed, but gradually his calm returned. He wondered what had gotten into Herdic. It puzzled him. Herdic had always been friendly towards Tincup. Mart knew that whatever the cause of Herdic's hostility, he had not lessened it this morning with his hasty blow. Yet at the slur Herdic had offered Rose, his temper, so long repressed, had flared violently. His actions

145

afterwards had been uncontrolled and instinctive. Scowling, he headed across the street towards the hotel, leaving his horse tied before the sheriff's office.

At the desk he asked: "Which room is Raoul's?"

When the man gave him the number, he turned toward the stairs. In the clerk, as in Herdic, Mart sensed a concealed animosity. Herdic had mentioned his treatment of Lucille. Could it be that Lucille had managed to gain the friendship and sympathy of the townspeople and had told a story of their trouble favorable to herself and unfavorable to him? He admitted that it was possible, even likely. She was an accomplished actress, so much so that she had easily fooled Mart. It would not be hard for her to play the part of a wronged wife.

A woman could put a man in a damned difficult position. Because he could not betray the fact that Rose had told him, he had this morning been obliged to conceal how he knew that Howie Frye was behind the attack on Raoul. Now he was obliged to accept the town's bitter judgment of him because decency would not allow him to air his quarrel with Lucille in public.

He shrugged and climbed the stairs. Raoul's door was open, and Mart could hear the old man's deep tones and, in reply, Rose's throaty, sweet ones. He barged in, hat in hand.

Rose's color was high, and Raoul's old eyes had a wicked gleam in them.

Mart grinned, asked: "What's he been telling you to make you blush like that?"

Rose's color deepened, and she kept her eyes on her shoes after that first, glad glance at Mart.

Raoul rasped: "Tellin' her there's a room ready for you and her at Tincup and to hell with the country's sharp-tongued gossips."

Mart murmured, "You're getting well, all right. Can you

146

get along without your nurse for a while?"

Raoul's head was swathed in bandages. His splinted leg lay stiff and rigid beneath the thin blanket. He nodded.

"Don't you ever let her go again, boy, or by Jupiter I'll bring her back for myself. I ain't so damned old but what I could put more sparkle in her eyes than you do."

Rose glanced at him appealingly. His bony hand came over and squeezed her arm.

He said: "Go on. Remember what I told you."

Mart followed Rose from the room.

He said: "I want to talk to you, but there's no place here. I'll hire a buggy."

She nodded wordlessly. She walked with him down the stairs and out into the muddy street. The only snow remaining in Cedar City was that which lay on the north side of the roofs. Rose's light hand on Mart's arm burned through his heavy sheepskin, seeming to leave its brand on the corded muscles on his forearm. Its heat spread through his body, and his excitement grew.

Trying to keep his emotion out of his voice, he asked, "What was it Raoul told you that he wanted you to remember?"

Rose was looking straight ahead. Her voice was scarcely audible.

"He said there had never been a divorce in the Joliffe family. But he said there would be now. He told me to hold on to you and make you happy until things could get straightened out."

Mart's voice was hoarse. "And what did you tell him?"

She looked up. Mart's blood ran scalding hot in his veins.

She said: "I told him that you would have to ask me."

Mart realized suddenly that they were at the livery barn, and he stopped before it. Old Sherman Dawson came down the dim, reeking alley between the stalls, glared at Mart, and

147

asked shortly, "What you want, Mister Joliffe?"

"A buggy, Sherm."

Again that hostility. Sherm had never called him Mr. Joliffe in his life. It was disturbing to Mart, who was friendly by nature, who liked to be liked. He frowned. The town's hostility had given him the answer to the question Rose had raised in his mind. But he did not speak until he had helped her into the buggy, until they had cleared the limits of the town. Then he spoke.

"I can't ask you that, Rose." He gripped the reins with his right hand, his knee with his left, and both hands were white from the strain. Suddenly he added, harshly, "Damn Raoul for a meddling old fool! I want you, Rose. But I won't have you that way. I won't have the country blaming you for what's happened and will happen between Lucille and me. I won't have them kicking your name around in the saloon like that of a dance hall girl!"

Her chin came up.

"And if I won't stay for less?"

Mart did not know why he should not feel wildly, gloriously happy, but he didn't.

He said: "Make your own terms. But stay. I can't let you go again, Rose."

She was smiling, showing him confidence that was heartening.

"All right. I'll stay . . . at the hotel . . . on your terms."

He hauled the buggy horse to a stop. The horse looked around at him inquiringly. Mart did not see him. He had Rose in his arms, and his lips were hard against hers.

Lucille had been able to stir him but never like this. This was wild and sweet. This made the savage, age-old hungers stir in the depths of his body. This would go on and on and never stop.

Almost sobbing, Rose broke free of his arms, her hands pushing fiercely against his chest. Her voice was the merest whisper.

"Stop it! Stop it! How can I stay at the hotel, how can I wait to be your wife when you do that to me?"

The buggy horse tossed his head and tugged at the reins. Mart turned him around, not trusting himself to speak. Then, Rose's voice spoke, and he marveled at its matter-of-factness. She had herself under control, but the memory of her passion lingered in Mart, stirred him tremendously. She was matter-of-fact, but her eyes were not. They burned hotly into his.

"There is more about Howie that I haven't told you, Mart."

"What is that?"

"He has stirred up the sheepmen near Tillman. They're going to move in on Tincup grass this spring."

Mart's face hardened.

"Don't they know what happened to Robineau?"

"I don't know. I don't know anything about it but what I heard and what I saw."

Swiftly she told him of seeing Howie in Tillman with the two gunmen, one of whom Mart had killed the day before. She told him of Mrs. Poulos, of Howie's trip to the Poulos ranch with his promise of grass. Finally, she told him the other thing, the thing he had to know.

"Howie isn't my father at all, Mart."

Tears of horror welled into her eyes as she thought of that awful night, that night when Howie, old, scrawny, clumsy, had taken her into his arms.

She said: "While you were on roundup, Howie told me he wasn't my father. He put his arms around me. He kissed me."

She began to cry, shuddering, shivering.

"Oh, Mart, it was awful! I thought of him as my father. I told him . . . he knew that I loved you."

Her shoulders shook, and she sobbed almost uncontrollably.

"I fought away. I picked up a chair and told him I'd hit him with it."

Her sobbing quieted. Mart sat cold faced at the reins, staring straight ahead. Anger ridged his jaw muscles, narrowed his eyes. Rose went on.

"Then he started cursing me, calling me names. He said he was going to kill you. I told him we were going to be married and he said, if I married you, he'd kill you before nightfall."

Mart halted the horse, looped the reins about his wrist, and drew Rose close. Her face was wet with her tears, and her body trembled.

He asked softly, "Why didn't you tell me?"

"What would you have done? Howie's threatened you before. You can't kill a man or put him in jail for making a threat. And I knew how Howie would have done it, Mart. From behind. From a dark alley. From ambush, like he did with Raoul.

"Mart, I know Howie. I ought to know him. I grew up in the same house with him. He never does anything openly. He slinks and sneaks around. Like this sheep business, getting Poulos to do his dirty work for him. Like with Raoul, getting a gunman to do it for him. He won't give up, Mart. As long as he lives, you'll be watching, watching every stranger and wondering if Howie sent him. You'll be afraid of the dark, afraid to ride alone."

She began to sob anew.

"And it's all over me . . . it's all my fault." Her voice ran on, hysterical, filled with her terror. "Even the bad feeling in town against you is Howie's doing. Pete Stoddard told me about it last night. Howie made it sound so logical that even Pete was doubtful."

Mart hauled the buggy horse to a halt. The buggy stood directly before the hotel.

He said: "Dry your tears, Rose. Go on back to Raoul. And

stop worrying about me. There's only one way to lick Howie now, and that's by beating Poulos and his sheepmen. When that's done, we'll find Howie and. . . ."

And what? Kill him? Try to force an antagonistic Herdic to put him in jail and charge him with attempted murder?

Perhaps the same questions were running through Rose's mind, but she left them unuttered. She was white, drawn. She got down from the buggy seat listlessly and tried to smile up at him.

She murmured, "Be careful, Mart?"

Then she was gone, running lightly up the steps to the wide hotel verandah.

Mart swung the buggy around in mid-street. He turned at the next corner, drew up before a small, yellow-frame house whose yard was beginning already to turn green. The air was damp and cold, the sun sterile and without much warmth, shining through an overcoat of moisture evaporated from the drenched earth.

He tied the horse to the cast-iron hitching post and climbed the steps to the porch. Lucille answered the door, surprised but instantly cautious.

"What do you want?"

"Just to tell you something."

He felt ill at ease with her, but he could not hate her.

"I'm going to divorce you. There will be a settlement, but you had better not contest it. And nothing had better happen to the child, or you'll leave Cedar City without a cent. Is that clear enough?"

"It's clear enough."

Her eyes were green, cold as winter ice on the Little Snake. She spoke almost thoughtfully.

"Have you ever thought that a woman can hold a gun? Have you ever considered how little strength it takes to pull a trigger?

151

I am still your wife. If you were dead, I'd inherit Tincup."

Mart laughed harshly.

"No, you wouldn't. Because Raoul is still alive, and Tincup is Raoul's until he dies. Was that what Howie had in mind the other day? Are you and Howie working this sheep scheme together?"

For an instant her eyes betrayed her. Mart was not sure, but he felt at that moment that his random shot had scored. Then the door slammed in his face, and he turned back towards the street.

Lucille had lived with her hate so long, he felt, that she was now capable of anything, even killing Mart, even killing Raoul. Raoul was helpless in his room at the hotel, and Lucille would always have admittance to his room since she was his daughter-in-law.

She wouldn't dare, said Mart's thoughts, but he could not believe them. Lucille would dare anything, and now, Mart was convinced, the consequences of her actions would have little deterring effect on her. She wanted to see Raoul, Mart, and Tincup in ruins. She would sacrifice her own life, if necessary, to accomplish it.

He slapped the back of the buggy horse and moved through the deep street mud toward the stable. He handed down the reins to Sherm Dawson at the stable and gave him a silver dollar. Then he walked back towards the sheriff's office where his horse was tied.

Chapter Sixteen

As he waited, Mart considered the odds in this battle for Tincup's survival looming ahead of him. He knew what a concentrated array of power the sheepmen could assemble, knew their wealth and their determination. He guessed that Howie's part would be active to the extent of providing a spearhead of gunslingers.

He could expect no support either from Herdic or from the townspeople, could on the contrary expect only opposition. His own cash resources were going to be very limited, for he had to anticipate the large cash payment he had promised Lucille and prepare for it. That would take all Tincup had, all they could reasonably expect to scrape together. It might be easier if he could keep the grass, for if Tincup was solvent and in possession of their range, any one of the country's banks would loan him money. But if he lost the grass. . . .

He paused near his horse and then on impulse swung over across the street, leaving his horse tied. He banged open the doors of Stoddard's Saloon. The place was nearly empty, but there were a couple of Tincup's 'punchers at the table, idly playing two-handed poker, a bottle between them. Mart paused by their table.

"Go over to the hotel and stay outside Raoul's door. Somebody wants him dead awful bad. It's up to you to see they don't get to him."

The two stood up. Mart hesitated a moment, wondering about what he had to tell them next. Finally he said it reluctantly.

"Keep Missus Joliffe out, too. Rose Frye and Doc are the only ones you're to let in. I'll send a couple of others down in the morning to relieve you."

He watched them go out. He wandered over to the bar, watching Pete Stoddard's expression carefully as Pete slid him a bottle and glass. Pete had always been a good friend of Tincup's. Now he clearly was not. He was not condemning, as Herdic had been, but there was a cool, detached air about him that told Mart as plainly as words could have done that he was reserving judgment.

Mart tossed off his drink and without a word swung around and headed for the door. There was an odd, wild tingling in the back of his head, a stirring of the old, slow anger he had been feeling lately.

Damn them! Damn them all! Damn Poulos and his greed, Howie and his acid hatred. Damn Lucille!

He swung to his saddle and yanked the horse around. His body rigid, he rode up the road towards home.

He stopped fighting the threat of violence in his mind. He had been a man who disliked violence, who preferred to live in peace. Now he would try another kind of living. They had pushed him far enough. He would learn the feel of a spitting Colt in his hand, would learn the sound that a rifle bullet can make when it strikes solid human flesh.

They wanted Tincup, did they? Well, they might take it in the end. But he'd damned well see that it cost them — cost them in sheep and human blood. He would see to it that Tincup grass was the most expensive land Poulos had ever bought.

Morning found Tincup's entire crew, except for the two Mart had dispatched as Raoul's guards in town, riding in the upper valley on Tincup's winter range. The sun was bright and clear. The snow atop the plateau was but a light thin covering now which would be gone by noon. The air was still and warm.

They rode to the very end of the canyon, where it climbed

in steep stages to the final barrier of rimrock, and began the slow ride down country, gathering as they went. On each side of the canyon half a dozen men rode the steep slopes, the shady draws, pushing cattle ahead of them. When a pair of riders would gather a dozen or more, they would push them onto the valley floor into the bunch that was slowly growing there, held by three of Tincup's older hands.

It was hard work for the horses, for the cattle were wild, filled with spring's fresh energy. Mart changed horses four times that day, roping a fresh mount each time out of the remuda that was loosely herded along behind the cattle. At nightfall they had, he judged, a thousand head.

These were driven in to the ranch and showed into the big holding corral there. One of the hands drove a hayrack out to one of the haystacks, loaded it, and brought it in to feed them.

The crew trooped to the bunkhouse, cheerful and boisterous. Mart halted with Floyd just outside, realizing that it was the first chance he'd had to talk to the foreman since he'd last talked to Rose.

Floyd asked: "How was Raoul?"

"All right. Floyd, the crew has got to know what we're up against. I guess they've got to know the trouble between Lucille and me as well, or they might form some opinions of their own like the people in town have. It don't seem decent for me to tell them. It don't seem right for a husband to talk against his wife. But you could tell them."

"All right."

Mart told Floyd then why Lucille had married him. He told Floyd that Lucille had threatened to kill her child, might even try to kill Raoul. He told him of Howie's agreement with Poulos, and what Tincup had to face as soon as the grass got green.

He was pleased at the hardening of Floyd's jaw muscles, at

the gleam of pure anticipation in the foreman's eyes.

Floyd said softly, "Boss, don't worry about the crew. When we get through with those sheep outfits, they'll know soon enough to stay off Tincup grass."

Floyd was sure, but Mart was not.

He said: "Floyd, Poulos's outfit is big . . . big as Tincup. He'll have half a dozen smaller outfits to help him. And I'm sure Howie will be in it, too, probably with a dozen hired hardcases. But tell the boys they're drawing fighting wages . . . double wages starting the first of May."

He headed for the house, headed for the lonely and solitary supper which Fu Ling would have ready. But before he reached it, he heard the howl of the crew from the bunkhouse, a howl of pure anticipation, a howl of gleeful approval.

He wondered how they would feel towards him a month from now, with very probably a third of their number dead. He wondered if there are any wages which will pay a man for risking and perhaps losing his life. And he wondered if he himself would survive, wondered if he did how he would settle with Lucille, how he could free himself to marry Rose.

In morning's early darkness the crew rolled out and ate. A wrangler brought in the remuda, and each man roped himself a mount from the bunch. By the time the first gray of frosty spring dawn lay over Tincup, the crew and Mart were in the saddle.

They turned the herd out into the open brush beyond the gate, and the cutting began. Springing cows, cows and calves, bulls, the weaker animals of all descriptions were cut out and headed back up the valley. Steers and heifers were held in a bunch. By nine o'clock the job was finished, and Floyd detailed a couple of men to drive this bunch to the top of the plateau.

They rode back up the valley and took up yesterday's job

where they had left off last night. The day passed. The roundup went on. At week's end they had cut through the herd and put everything on top the plateau that was strong enough to stand the temporary shortage of grass.

There were no holidays, no Sundays, during roundup. The work continued from dawn to dark, seven days a week. The calf branding commenced. The days turned hot, and it seemed to Mart that the grass grew visibly every day. They would gather a bunch of two or three hundred, hold them in a tight group while riders roped cut calves, dragged them to the fire, put Tincup's brand on their hips, earmarked them, castrated, and vaccinated.

The air was filled with the stench of burning hair and flesh, of acrid wood smoke — with the reek of sweat, the raucous bawling of calves and cows, the shouted curses of men. And now, at each day's end, the herd handled that day was brought to the ranch, corralled, and on the following morning driven up the steep trail to the top of the plateau. Spring and fall were the hard-working times, and this was spring.

But as mid-April came, Mart began to feel uneasy about Poulos. One morning he approached Floyd as the foreman was washing in the icy water from the pump.

"I've been stewing about Poulos. It's early for sheep on top, but he might risk the loss of a few lambs to get the jump on us."

Floyd dried his face briskly and ran a piece of comb through his stiff, graying hair.

He said: "Want to take a look today?"

Mart nodded.

"You and me. That won't stop the branding and, if we find anything, we can come back for the crew before we jump into it."

After breakfast Mart strapped on his Colt, emptied a box

157

of shells for his rifle into his pocket, and took the gun from its place behind the kitchen door. He found Floyd waiting, similarly armed, and the two turned the cow and calf herd out of the corral and started it towards the trail.

By taking up this herd as they went out on top, they would save a morning's work for two men so that their scouting ride would deprive the branding crew of but two men for only half a day. At nine they pushed the last of the slow-moving herd up through the rim and rode out on top in warm April sunlight.

Already the grass was two inches high. In the shady draws quakies were leafing out, their young, new leaves the palest green. An occasional wild flower bloomed against the ground. Sage chickens, invisible in the low brush, started out from under their horses' hoofs, never failing to make the animals shy violently.

Foreboding — a strange feeling to come over a man in warm, bright sunlight — began to stir in Mart.

Floyd, riding behind, asked: "How you figure they'll hit us? You think they'll come up in one big bunch with all their guards on it, or in small bunches, scattered out?"

Mart frowned. He had been considering the same problem himself. He spoke his thoughts aloud, musing.

"Howie doesn't know that Rose spilled his plans. He knows how Robineau's sheep bothered me last spring. I think he's counting on me hesitating because of that."

"Then he'd put small bunches up, try to make us think each one was independent of the other."

Mart nodded.

Floyd, looking out ahead towards the horizon, asked: "What are you goin' to do? You paid pretty high for what we did to Robineau's sheep. You going to let that string halter you?"

Mart scowled. He had been wondering himself how he would

handle this crisis when it arose. He had told himself a hundred times that utter firmness was all that could conceivably achieve his purpose. He thought of Robineau, brazenly moving in on grass that did not belong to him. He considered the man's cowardice in killing himself after he had been defeated, and the subsequent vengeance which Lucille had wrought against Mart because of it. He thought of Howie, of the pain he had suffered all winter because of the bullets of Howie's hired killer. He thought of Raoul, even now crippled, also because of Howie.

He said: "No."

But there was no real conviction in the word. Mart seriously wondered if it were in him to ride into a camp of sheep herders, guns spitting, cutting them down. He wondered, and his foreboding increased.

Floyd looked at him doubtfully.

He growled: "There ain't but one way to handle this, Mart, and you know it. You drive them off, or they drive you. You kill them, or they kill you. You ain't worried about Herdic?"

Mart could be no less than honest.

"He's hostile to Tincup because of Lucille and the stories she's told around town. I can't do any fighting from a cell in Herdic's jail."

"Let the sheep outfits fire the first shot. Then you're in the clear."

The morning passed. Steadily riding, they came at noon to the squat, sod-roofed cabin that was Tincup's line camp. Mart corralled the horses, and Floyd built a fire in the tiny stove. They boiled coffee, opened a can of beans. There was evidence of previous occupancy here, dirty plates, a dirty skillet.

Floyd commented: "We'd better ride careful this afternoon."

Mart gulped his beans, drank his scalding coffee. He wished he could rid himself of his hesitancy. He wondered what he would do when he rode up to one of Poulos's sheep camps today. He was hoping that they would make the first overt move and thus release him from the reluctance that was torturing him.

And for the first time the deep-seated question that had unconsciously bothered him for a month came to the surface. *What will it do to me? I stewed for months over killing Robineau's sheep. What will I feel when I look at the bodies of men I've killed?* His squirming mind argued with itself. *What did you feel when you killed the man who shot Raoul? Nothing. Why, then, should you feel more guilt over these?*

He knew the answer to that. The great majority of the men Tincup had to fight were guilty of nothing but taking their pay for doing their jobs. Howie's gunmen would bother him little, he knew. But how about the little men, the sheep herders? He wondered how Raoul would be if faced with the same decision and knew the answer to that without hesitation. There was no softness in Raoul.

Floyd finished washing the dishes, carried his wash water to the door, and dumped it out. Mart shaped a cigarette, touched a match to its end, and went out the door. Floyd picked up his rifle and followed.

Up on the hillside, in a patch of dark spruce timber, Ben Corbin was lying prone. He raised his rifle, rested the barrel against the trunk of a tree, and drew a bead on Mart's chest. The range was long — three hundred yards. Corbin stilled his breathing and felt the muzzle of the gun steady in his hands. Mart was moving towards the corral now, presenting the narrower target of his side to Corbin's eyes.

The muzzle of the gun followed inexorably. Mart caught his horse and led him out of the corral. Corbin softly cursed. Mart stood behind the horse and threw up the saddle, stooped slightly to cinch it down.

Floyd rose to his saddle, his horse dancing, and then Mart followed suit. Mart headed uphill toward the ambush, Floyd riding beside him. Corbin waited. He could hear the rustle that Howie Frye and the others made, coming up behind him. His finger tightened down on the trigger. He spoke to Howie behind him.

"Two shots, and we make an end to this scrap. Raoul's dead. There's Mart and his foreman. I've got Mart in my sights. You take the foreman, and the war is over. Tincup can't fight without a leader."

He stopped his breathing and squeezed. A flurry of motion beside him made little impression upon his consciousness until Howie's boot struck his rifle barrel just as it discharged. The bullet tore up dust a foot to one side of Mart, and his horse jumped.

Corbin rolled, coming to his feet, his face a mask of rage. Before he could speak, Howie fairly screamed: "Who's giving the orders around here, you or me?"

Poulos's heavy voice cut in.

"Neither of you. I'm the one that gets the grass, and I'm giving the orders. Cut 'em down, boys."

His gun muzzle poked into Howie's back.

Mart and Floyd were down off their horses. They were hidden in the low brush of the hillside. One of their rifles barked, and a bullet thudded into the trunk of a tree, three feet from Corbin's head. He ducked.

Howie's voice was taut and sharp.

"I told you I was going to run this show. I don't want Joliffe dead. I want to see him squirm. I want to see him broke, and then I want to kill him myself."

Corbin snapped a shot down at a brush clump on the hillside. It raised an angry shout and an answering shot that ricocheted off a rock at his feet and whined away.

Poulos said: "Corbin, take three men and circle around. Get them in a crossfire."

Corbin crept away, three of his hard-faced companions following. Poulos's voice was dry, without emotion, as he spoke to the others.

"Keep firing. Keep them pinned down there until Corbin can get around."

Howie Frye was white, trembling with rage. Corbin heard a shot that was oddly muffled as he moved away and turned his head in puzzlement. Howie was clutching a bloody, spreading stain on his dirty shirt front, and Poulos, behind him, was smiling strangely, his eyes bright with some inner satisfaction. As Howie fell, Poulos shoved his gun into his holster, backed away and followed Corbin through the heavy screen of timber.

Chapter Seventeen

Down on the hillside Mart hugged the ground, white with sudden, murderous rage. All of his doubts were gone, and he could wonder now why he had ever entertained doubt in the first place. He was not fighting ordinary men. He was fighting thieves — grass thieves and killers. He was fighting Howie Frye. He was fighting chill-eyed gunmen who would stop at nothing — neither at murdering an old man from ambush nor at murdering Floyd and himself in the same way.

Floyd lay behind a clump of sarvus a dozen feet away. Two weeks earlier in the season this brush would have afforded little or no protection. Now, however, with its new green covering of young leaves, the brush made an impenetrable screen. Impenetrable to the eye — not to a bullet.

As Mart had come off his horse, he'd shown the presence of mind to snatch his rifle from the boot. Floyd had not. Now, Mart fumbled in his pocket for a handful of rifle shells and shoved them into the magazine of the carbine. With the rifle loaded, he holstered his Colt.

Floyd called softly, "Hit, Mart?"

"No. How about you?"

"I'm all right. But we're in a bad spot. They'll circle after a bit and put us in a crossfire."

For an instant the impulse was strong in Mart to leap up and run, but he controlled it with an effort. He had often wondered what it would be like to face certain death, had wondered if he would feel fear. He admitted now that he would probably have been afraid if he were not so damned mad. He was not ready to die. Perhaps he would never be ready. Life was a sweet and precious thing to any man, even when his life was as much a personal maelstrom as was Mart's. No, he felt no fear, only a raging, futile anger because he knew that they would kill him, because they would take Tincup's grass, because they would win and he would lose.

The horses had halted uncertainly a hundred feet away. Gunfire had disturbed them, had made them nervous but, with some distance between them and the guns now, they were calmed and began to munch grass.

Beyond the horses was a shallow ravine, a dry water course which in rainy weather carried away the runoff. Mart thought: *If we could reach that. . . .* He shook his head. It would but postpone the inevitable, for without horses they could not hope to escape. He gave some consideration to a dash for the ravine, a grab at the horses as they went, but again shook his head. The horses were skittish from the shooting. They would not be too easily caught. They would fidget and move away, trailing their reins if a man approached them.

He shrugged. A bullet probed through the brush behind which he hid and a twig, cut by its passage, dropped into his upturned face. Rolling, he poked his rifle ahead of him, snapped a shot at Corbin above him in the trees. He heard the ricochet of the bullet into space, a dim, receding whine. *Missed!*

A rain of bullets kicked up dust beside and before him. He ducked back hastily.

Floyd called: "Got any ideas?"

"I was thinking about that ravine, but it's a hundred and fifty feet away. Even if we did reach it, it wouldn't do any good. It would just postpone things a little."

He heard a muffled pistol shot from above and was puzzled at this. They had rifles up there, and this range was nearly two hundred yards, hardly the range for a revolver.

He swung his glance to the right and knew instantly from what direction the next shots would come. The timber in which the ambushers hid ran along the crest of this ridge for a couple of hundred yards then petered out on a high point which looked directly down upon the two hidden men. If they switched their position enough to conceal themselves from that vantage point, they would then become exposed to the other.

He peered around the brush clump and stared at the timber above. He thought he saw a man crawling, but the target was too uncertain, too fleeting. The man appeared to be crawling out of the timber and into the brush, traveling at a slight downhill tangent. Mart was puzzled. Surely none of them would try an open, creeping attack through the brush when the other method was so sure.

He watched the place where the man had disappeared, following his apparent course through the brush by the faintly waving tops of the bushes. He frowned.

The man was not even heading towards Mart and Floyd. He was, instead, following a course which would put him between Mart and the flanking party.

Mart muttered to Floyd, pointing, "What the hell's he doing?"

"I dunno. Cut down on him."

"Can't see him long enough at a time."

The minutes ran on, each one a sweating, tortured eternity. At last Mart saw a stir in the timber where it petered out on the point. He tried to edge around so as to cover himself partially from both places. He called to Floyd.

"Here it comes."

From directly above bullets poured into their position. Mart rolled to escape, his eyes covering the ground to his left as he did so. Something strange about that glimpse disturbed him, but he could not for a moment tell what it was. But suddenly he knew.

He whispered, "Floyd, the horses are gone. You see where they went?"

Floyd looked. His eyes were puzzled as he turned back towards Mart.

"They sure got away fast."

Sudden hope shot through Mart. He said excitedly: "Floyd, they didn't run away! They just went into that shallow ravine!"

A crackle of rifle fire burst from the point off to the right. The moment they had dreaded arrived at last, with a wicked, murderous crossfire pouring into their position.

Floyd grunted as a bullet grazed his arm. He said sharply: "Mart, we ain't going to lay here an' let 'em cut us to bits. We've got to get out of here. I'd as soon be shot runnin', tryin' to get away, as shot layin' here on my belly like a snake."

"Hell, you won't make it, Floyd, but try it if you want to. I can't cover both places at once, but I'll do the best I can for you. Wait 'til I load up this rifle. If I can keep the lead flying fast enough, you could make it, I suppose. If you get there, you catch the horses first, and cover me while I make a dash for it."

It wouldn't work. If there were but two or three men shooting at them, it might be different. But a man had little chance when eight to a dozen guns were spitting at him. Floyd would run perhaps a third of the distance before they cut him down. After that, Mart would have to lie and listen to bullets thud into Floyd's inert body, knowing that all chance was gone, that death was but seconds away.

If only the horses had wandered into the ravine at the very beginning! Then they might have had a chance, for Mart believed he could have kept the ambushers harassed enough in their single position so that accurate shooting at Floyd would have

166

been impossible. He knew, too, that he could never pour enough lead into both widely separated positions to keep them from getting Floyd.

He had forgotten the lone man crawling through the brush, but suddenly he remembered. He felt a sudden chill in his body. What if the man changed directions? What if he were now but short yards away, drawing a bead on Mart's head?

He raised his head the barest fraction and peered into the screen of low brush. But he saw nothing. He rose himself as far as he could without exposing his head and body too recklessly.

He said to Floyd: "I'm ready when you are."

He could sense the slight movement as Floyd gathered his feet under him, as he crouched ready to run. A hundred and fifty feet to run, a hundred and fifty rough, exposed feet.

He turned his head, and the words started from his lips, "Floyd! Don't do it! You'll never. . . ."

But Floyd was up. It was as though a hundred rifles had opened up all at once. Mart stood up, feeling that at least he could draw a part of their fire away from Floyd. Bullets showered around him, glancing off the ground and whining eerily away. And then his rifle was at his shoulder, and he was pouring a murderous, concentrated fire into the position above him.

For a seemingly endless moment Howie Frye's mind was stunned, too occupied with the horror of the thing that had happened to him to understand fully its consequences. He felt as though some terrible force had smashed him from behind. Then the pain struck excruciatingly, greater than any Howie had ever felt before.

The front of him was suddenly soaked and hot. Automatically he clutched himself with both hands, felt the slickness of fresh, warm blood, felt, too, the bulging of his entrails at the gaping hole. He knotted his hands and pressed them back, Then he was falling. Consciousness slipped away from him. His brain reeled, and the earth whirled before his eyes.

He hardly felt the impact as he hit the ground. His brain was fighting, was feebly clutching at consciousness while it shouted, *This is wrong! You're being cheated. They're going to kill Mart, and that will be too easy for him. You've been double-crossed!*

It seemed a very long time before his body responded to the frantic urging of his brain, but at last sharp, clear consciousness returned. He was going to die. He then thought of Mart and Floyd, pinned down on the slope. He thought of Anthony Poulos, grizzled, thick set, dark skinned. He knew that he had underestimated Poulos's ruthlessness and determination. He had made a fatal mistake.

Too late to strike back at Poulos, but perhaps not too late to thwart him. He tried to raise his head, but it fell back. He concentrated all the force and virulence of his hatred for Mart on the task. He felt the quickened beat of his heart, a faint surge of strength to his muscles. He raised his head again and peered down the slope. He turned his head and looked behind him.

Poulos was gone. So was Corbin, and so were a couple of the others. The attention of those that remained was fixed on the slope below. No one noticed Howie, half hidden in the screen of low brush that covered the ground here in the timber.

Fuzziness clutched at him. It would have been so easy to lie back, to let the delicious languor seize him, to let the drug of pain overcome him. But there was Mart, down on the hillside. There was Howie's acid hatred of him. Howie wanted him to die — but not yet. Howie wanted him to suffer first.

No longer could he remember why he hated Mart. He only knew that he did. He hated Mart more than he loved life. And if he could prevent Poulos from killing Mart, he might yet satisfy that hatred, could feel as he died that Mart would suffer the loss of his grass, of Tincup, before he himself was killed.

Howie's hand still clutched his rifle. Carefully he eased himself down the slope, carefully so that none of those left above him could see. As he crawled, the life ran out of him in a scarlet stream and left its trail on the ground behind him.

He had started at first with no plan, straight down the slope towards Mart. He had hardly gone a dozen feet when he realized that this was wrong. He could be of no help to Mart by crawling to him. Mart would shoot him, and that would be that.

He struggled with the nausea and faintness that strove to overcome him. Poulos — Corbin — the others. Where had they gone? Then from out of his unconscious mind came the half remembered words of Poulos to Corbin, "Corbin, take three men and circle around. Get them in your crossfire."

That was the most dangerous threat to Mart at the moment — that crossfire. Howie did not know how a single, mortally wounded man could stop that crossfire, but he could try. There was most certainly nothing else he could do.

His eyes scanned the timber above him, noted the place where it petered out on a high point, and recognized that spot as the only logical vantage point for the flanking party.

He crawled for an endless time and at last, reaching a fairly clear spot, raised his head and peered around. He could see Mart from here, prone on the ground, could see one of Floyd's feet beyond Mart. He looked past Floyd and saw the shallow ravine. He thought, *Why the hell don't they break and run for that?*

Then he saw Floyd gather his feet under him, saw him crouch, and get ready to run. He saw Mart, looking around, his face wild and raging.

He knew then that they were going to do it. Poulos and

Corbin opened up from the point, and the bullets sang softly over Howie's head. They had not seen him.

He saw Floyd leap to his feet and begin his run. He saw Mart levering shells into his rifle, firing, levering again, shooting into the fringe of timber above him.

Suddenly Howie knew what he could do, knew what he had to do if he were to succeed in thwarting Poulos. Mart could not cover both parties of attackers at once. He could cover only the one above him. But Howie could cover the flanking party, could pin them down so that their fire would be ineffective.

He could grasp Mart's strategy. Somehow the horses had wandered into that gully. If Floyd reached it, he would then cover Mart until Mart could reach it too.

Howie pulled himself around, rolled, and came to a sitting position. Now he had to take his one hand away from the torn and gaping wound in his belly. The hand was slick and slippery against the rifle stock. He levered the rifle and raised it to his shoulders. Pain shot through him, and he could feel his entrails pouring out of the wound.

Poulos and Corbin stood exposed, firing down over him. If they saw him, they gave no sign. Howie aimed at Poulos and pulled the trigger. Poulos howled, slapped his thigh as though a bee had stung him there, and then jumped down to crouch behind a boulder. Howie fired at Corbin, missed. But Corbin joined Poulos behind the rock.

For the barest fraction of a minute there was no fire at all from that quarter. Then Corbin poked his rifle around the boulder and fired. The bullet tore through the brush beside Howie's head.

He jerked his head aside, threw up his rifle, and shot at Corbin's head. He knocked a shower of rock splinters into Corbin's face, heard the man's shouted curse.

Firing suddenly halted behind him, and he risked a glance over his shoulder. Mart was crouched again, grinning out of a sweaty, dusty face.

Howie felt a stir of satisfaction. Floyd had made it, then, for Mart would not be grinning if he had not.

It did not seem strange now to Howie that he, who hated Mart more than anything else in life, should be helping him. His twisted mind had convinced itself that in this way his revenge against Mart could be greater, could be more satisfying. And he entertained no doubt that Poulos would kill Mart in the end. That was inevitable, particularly now that he knew how ruthless and cold Poulos could be. So let Mart live to suffer the loss of Tincup and then let Poulos have him if he would.

A shot banged out from the ravine. Mart jumped up and began to run, weaving and twisting, leaping brush, ducking low. A crackle of fire broke out from above, and the rifle in the ravine stepped up its tempo. A howl came from the high fringe of timber, and a hasty glance showed Howie a man, out in the open, staggering downhill, his eyes glazed and dull with pain.

Howie jerked himself around and threw his own rifle to his shoulder. He had automatically loaded the weapon during the lull while Floyd got set in the ravine. Now he peppered the boulder behind which Poulos and Corbin crouched. And he kept feeding fresh shells into the magazine.

Desperation was in Poulos now. He leaped into the open, Corbin behind him, and drew a bead on the running Mart. Howie slammed a hasty shot at him just as he fired. Howie fired again, and Corbin's legs went out from under him. Poulos howled at the others who were cautiously shooting from behind the screen of timber, and they reluctantly stepped into the open and raised their rifles. Howie levered and shot, levered and shot.

Suddenly the gun in the ravine was silent. Dismay touched Howie, but then he heard the thunder of frantic hoofs, and the two horses, bearing Mart and Floyd, thundered down the ravine, out onto the open valley floor where Tincup's line camp squatted, and at last disappeared into the timber behind it.

Howie saw Poulos running down towards him. He sought to raise his rifle, to bring the man down. But his life lay as a stain on the ground between here and the timber fringe. His life had run out slowly through the hole in his belly and, when Poulos reached him, he was dead.

Chapter Eighteen

There was a time, during the supper hour at the hotel in Cedar City, when the lobby was almost deserted. The clerk got himself a plate from the kitchen and retired into his office cubbyhole to eat it. From past observation, Lucille knew that nothing short of a riot would bring him out until he had finished.

Raoul and Rose, like most people, were creatures of habit. At exactly seven every night they came down the wide staircase and went into the dining room, Raoul hobbling along on his crutches, Rose walking slightly behind him.

Therefore, when Lucille came into the hotel tonight, she was wholly unobserved. She hurried to the stairs and ran, panting, up to the second floor. She was now quite plainly pregnant and had taken to wearing voluminous dresses, full at the waist partially to conceal her condition. Without hesitation, she went directly to Raoul's room, opened the door, and slipped inside.

Rose had opened the window for the purpose of airing out the room while she and Raoul were at dinner. Soft light filtered in from outside, making the outlines of furniture barely discernible. Lucille did not light the lamp.

She walked to the window and stared down. The window opened onto a vacant lot next to the hotel, but there was a narrow ledge of shingled roof, perhaps two feet wide, just below the window. A person might stand on that ledge, but it was definitely not a means of egress from the hotel. It led nowhere.

Now that she had irrevocably embarked upon this course, she felt a nervous fear in the pit of her stomach. She felt a rising nausea, but she had become accustomed to nausea in the past months. From her bodice she withdrew the small pistol she had bought, the one with which she had practiced so assiduously these last two weeks.

It was a Colt Derringer, a .41 caliber Cloverleaf model, holding four bullets. It nestled in her hand, cold and compact and very deadly. Lucille smiled shakily. Fear churned in her stomach.

Many times in the past year she had wished she could kill. Tonight was the first time she had actually come to the point of attempting it. Something had to stop the torment her life had become. If she accepted the money Mart had offered, she would have to give up her child. If she refused the money and fled with the baby, she would have no means of supporting the two of them.

She was aware that by now Anthony Poulos and Howie Frye must surely be moving sheep onto Tincup's grass. She knew that when they did, Mart would fight and, when he fought, he would very likely be killed on the spot. If Mart were to die before Raoul did, then Lucille would be out in the cold as far as Tincup was concerned. She was determined that this could not be allowed to happen to her and to her child.

She was Mart Joliffe's wife. She felt that she had suffered enormously at his hands. When he died, Tincup should go to her, and she knew that only by this means could she insure it.

The room seemed excessively cold to her. She began to tremble violently. She exerted all the power of her will to still her shaking body, for she knew she could not hold the pistol steady if her hands were trembling.

Seconds were hours, minutes eternities. She sat down and tried to relax. Then she stood up and paced the floor. She went to the window a dozen times. She looked at the door longingly, and once crossed to it and almost opened it. Fear told her to leave. Determination and her need to secure a life for her child made her stay. Hate was no longer part of her. Desperation had replaced it.

At last she heard steps in the hall, voices approaching. They halted just outside the door. Rose was speaking, her voice a soft murmur through the door's thickness.

"Good night, Raoul. You'll be going home soon."

"Not without you. Damn it, Rose, I've told you he was going to get a divorce from her. Why won't you come home to Tincup when I go?"

"You know the reason," Rose replied wearily. "We've been over it all a dozen times."

"Well, come in a while anyway. There's nothin' on earth so damned lonely as a hotel room."

Raw panic stirred in Lucille while Rose hesitated. If Rose came in, she was lost. She knew she could not kill them both, for she was a match for neither of them physically. Besides that, while she felt that no jury would convict her for killing Raoul in view of the sympathy Howie had stirred up in town for her, she was fully aware that killing Rose would be quite another matter.

Rose asked: "Will you promise not to try to change my mind?"

Suddenly Lucille knew that Rose would agree. She knew she was lost. Her eyes drifted frantically around the room, seeking a place to hide. The closet would not do, for they would undoubtedly hang up their coats as soon as they came in. The bed . . . ? Suddenly Lucille recalled the small roof ledge below the window.

With no further hesitation she ran to it, lifted her skirts, and put one leg through. When she felt the firmness of the shingled roof beneath her foot, she put her weight on it, drew her body through, and then pulled the other foot after her. She moved aside just as the door opened, just as the room was lighted from the dim lamps in the hall.

Lucille saw the flare as Rose struck a match, and a moment later the soft light of the lamp filled the room, cast its glow on the roof outside. Lucille drew herself back against the hotel wall. She still clutched the Derringer in her hand. She heard Rose's shivering exclamation of chill, and she came over to close the window. Lucille was no more than three feet from her, and it seemed impossible that Rose would not see her. But apparently Rose did not, for she closed the window and moved back into the room.

Panic raced through Lucille. The window was closed, and she did not know whether she could open it from the outside or not. She had no way of knowing how long Rose would stay with Raoul. She had successfully eluded Raoul's guards, had placed herself in his room, but all of her careful planning had been upset simply because he was lonely and wanted Rose to come in and talk.

Lucille looked down at the ground, perhaps fifteen feet below the level of her eyes, and shuddered violently. It took all her determination to raise her glance, to overcome the dizziness that whirled in her brain.

She looked to right and left, seeking an escape elsewhere. Raoul's room was located in a gable and, from both sides of the gable, the roof raised steeply to its peak. Further back towards the alley the hotel was, however, a full two stories, and there the windows of the rooms made a solid line. But there was no roof ledge beneath them for Lucille to walk upon.

Even in April there was a chill in the air at nightfall, perhaps more penetrating because of the closeness of the Little Snake River. And there is something about fear and nervous tension that has its chilling effect upon the human body.

Lucille suddenly realized that she was icy cold all through her body. Her teeth chattered with her shivering. Her knees wobbled and threatened to betray her, to give out beneath her.

In what had become a frenzy she knew that she would have to get back into Raoul's room or fall to the ground below. She was becoming weaker, and she could feel the waves of dizziness rising in her head. She knew now the bitterness of defeat. Hate returned and united with her desperation. She hated all men suddenly, not just Mart and Raoul, but all men — because physically they were strong, and she was weak.

A man would have no trouble waiting out here on this roof ledge until Rose and Raoul finished their talk, and Rose returned to her own room. For a man, that would have been easy.

And then, in that instant, a new ray of hope filtered into Lucille's mind. She still clutched the Derringer in her hand. It was of steel, hard and solid. She could, if she were careful, break out the window with it, fire and kill Raoul before Rose could interfere. Afterwards, she knew the tension of today and tonight would burst the dam of control in her. She would be tearful, hysterical, repentant.

Pregnant women sometimes did strange things, had strange emotional upheavals. She did not believe that a person in Cedar City would fail to understand and forgive her action. None — except perhaps Rose.

Carefully she eased herself around until, instead of facing the brink, she faced the wall. Then she began her side-stepping movement along the ledge toward the window. Unfortunately, she stood to the left of the window, and that meant that she would have to ease along in front of the window to its right side so that her right hand, the hand which held the gun, would be in a position to break the window and fire at Raoul.

She peered in. Raoul sat not four feet from the window, his back to her. Rose sat across the room, lightly poised on a straight-backed chair. Lucille smiled faintly with satisfaction. Had she directed their seating herself, she could not have done it more perfectly. She knew that her aim with this small gun might be faulty. At the range of the room's full width, she might very probably have missed. Yet at a distance of four feet. . . .

Still smiling lightly, she crouched and began to inch her way past the window. A shingle, old and cracked, loosened from the roof, slipped beneath her feet.

Panic touched her, but her left hand went down to the ledge, and she steadied herself. Slowly, with her heart pounding madly, she continued, until at last she could stand again, could look into the window again.

The soft murmur of their talk reached her ears. She hesitated for a moment more, waiting for the fright of her near fall to wear off, for her shivering knees to steady.

Then, tense and hardly breathing, she raised the Derringer. Its barrel came against the glass of the window, and it shattered with a loud crash, followed by a light tinkling as the pieces of broken pane clattered inside the room.

Rose sprang from her chair, utter shock and amazement mirrored in her features. Raoul started to turn, but he could not rise from his chair without the crutches which lay now on the bed.

Gaunt and old, thought Lucille. Ready to die. She leveled the Derringer, pointed it at the middle of his back, and thumbed back the hammer. Her finger tightened on the spur trigger. But the force of her straining, as she smashed the window, had loosened a shingle beneath her feet. She felt it slip, and clutched at the window for support. The gun wavered and discharged. Lucille's hand encountered the broken glass of the window, and the sharp edges bit deeply. The shingle slipped again, and suddenly Lucille screamed. Then she was falling, back, out into thin air — falling towards the ground a dozen feet away.

It seemed a very long time before she struck. Then there

was pain, terrible, crippling pain in her abdomen, a terrific shortage of air in her lungs. Wildly gasping for air, she thought: *The child! I've killed my child!*

It was then that she realized the full force of defeat, for she knew she had missed Raoul. She knew as well that her hold over Mart Joliffe was gone. She tried to get up but could do nothing save moan and gasp, and at last, mercifully, she fainted.

The first thing Rose did was to run to Raoul, to throw herself at his feet, and exclaim anxiously: "Are you all right?"

He nodded, somewhat dazedly.

Rose caught her breath then.

"Lucille will need the doctor."

She started for the door, saw Raoul's crutches on the bed, snatched them, and gave them to him. Then she fled out of the room and down the stairs.

The clerk was standing at the staircase, looking up.

He asked: "What's the matter? Was it you that screamed? Where did that shot come from?"

Behind Rose, closely behind, came the two Tincup 'punchers who were Raoul's guards.

Rose commanded: "Go back and help Raoul." To the clerk she said: "Get the doctor at once. Missus Joliffe fell from the window of Raoul's room."

The clerk looked his plain disbelief, but Rose had not time for further explanations.

She said sharply: "The doctor. You fool, the doctor!"

Then she was out of the door, running around the corner of the hotel.

Lucille lay sprawled in the weeds below Raoul's window. Rose knelt beside her and picked up her left hand to chafe the wrist. The hand was covered with blood, sticky with it,

179

where Lucille had cut herself on the broken window. The gun lay three feet from her outstretched right hand.

For an instant Rose was tempted to conceal the gun. Then she thought of the suffering the woman had caused Mart, of the thing she had just now tried to do. She considered that without the motive of murder, Lucille's fall would be very hard to explain and, in the town's present temper, highly embarrassing to both Raoul and herself. People would ask, "How come she fell? Somebody push her? Were you three fightin' up there?" No. The truth would best serve everyone concerned.

Joe Herdic, who seemed to sense it whenever there was trouble in Cedar City, who could hear a gunshot farther than anyone else, came around the corner, his revolver in his fist. He holstered it at once and hurried to where Rose knelt beside Lucille. His glance took in the gun instantly then lifted to the broken window.

He said: "She didn't fall out that window. The hole ain't big enough. What happened?"

Rose murmured, "She must have been outside on that ledge. The window broke, and there she was, with that gun in her hand. She fired once at Raoul, but she must have slipped, because she screamed and fell."

She stood up as she saw Doc Saunders approaching.

Doc saw who it was and grumbled immediately: "Only cases of violence I've had in a year have been the Joliffes. She fall out of that window?"

Herdic mumbled, "Off the ledge."

He picked up the tiny Derringer, looked at it, smelled the bore, then dropped it into his pocket. There was a fair-size crowd gathered around now, their faces white and shocked.

Doc got to his feet, saying, "Couple of you go fetch a door. Hurry it up. She's about four months along. Ain't much chance of savin' the child."

He fished his pipe from his pocket, stuck it in his mouth,

and sucked noisily on the stem. Then he put it away. Two men came running with a door out of the hotel and laid it down beside Lucille. Doc moved her gently onto it, first her head, then her feet.

He said: "All right. Pick it up and bring it into the hotel."

The two men lifted the door, one in front, one behind, and carried it up the steps to the hotel verandah. Doc walked beside them, steadying Lucille. Lucille moaned and stirred as they carried her through the door. Herdic faced the crowd.

He said: "Mart ain't said a word in his own defense. He ain't likely to, I guess. I think I'll say one for him.

"I ain't going to talk against his wife. She's hurt and, if she ain't paid for what she done before, she's payin' now. Tonight she tried to kill Raoul. Looks to me now like we might have been a mite hard on Mart."

Rose looked at the sheepish faces of the crowd. Herdic stumped down the steps of the verandah and crossed towards his office. Rose went inside.

Raoul was in the lobby. He was hard and fierce, as always, yet tonight Rose thought she detected a bit of puzzled regret in him.

He muttered, "I'll be damned if it don't beat the Dutch how much can come out of some simple little thing. Robineau runs his sheep in on us, trying to make a little steal stick. We only do what we might reasonably be expected to do, an' look what happens."

Rose was thinking, *Howie's to blame for a lot of this trouble,* but she said nothing.

Raoul sat down and propped his crutches against the wall beside him.

Then Rose murmured, "I ought to go up and see her. She is in for a bad time. Another woman might help."

Raoul grunted, unsmilingly. "You're like Mart. You've got

a soft streak in you." Then his severity lightened, and he gave her a small smile. "It becomes a woman. Maybe it becomes a man sometimes, too. Mart felt pretty bad about those sheep. I didn't let on, but I could see it. He felt guilty about Robineau."

He stared at Rose, but for once he did not seem to see her.

"Maybe Mart's the one that's right. Maybe I'm the one that's wrong. This is the first time I've realized it, I guess, but there ought to be a way to settle an argument short of shootin' it out or drivin' another man's stock off a rim."

Rose stood up and squeezed his hand, smiling.

"We're what we are. The Lord made us that way."

"Doc took her to my room," he said, answering her unspoken question.

Rose ran lightly up the stairs, but she slowed as she approached Raoul's room. This was foolish and useless, perhaps. Lucille could feel nothing but hate for Rose. She would be bitter, perhaps even vindictive. Still, she was all alone, except for gruff Doc Saunders.

Rose tapped lightly at the door, and Doc rumbled, "Come in."

Lucille was conscious, but her face was twisted with agony. Doc turned, saw Rose, and seemed relieved.

He said, "Labor pains. She's having a miscarriage." His voice held a certain resentment. "She's weak. She ain't et all winter like I've told her to. She's been livin' on hate and misery, and so she's weak."

Rose pulled a chair to the bedside opposite Doc and sat down. She found Lucille's knotted fist, straightened it out, and took it in her own. She looked at Lucille, saw the ravages that bitterness and sorrow and desperation had left. She knew this woman had all but ruined Mart, but she could not hate Lucille. She could only feel unbearably sad.

182

Lucille's fingers clenched tightly against Rose's, until Rose thought her hand would be crushed. Sweat beaded the red-haired woman's face. A groan escaped through her pale lips, her clenched teeth.

Time went on — time and the tiny woman's agony. But it was over at last. It was over when Doc drew the sheet up over Lucille's thin and ravaged face. And then Rose wept.

Chapter Nineteen

When they gained the shelter of the trees and the rifle slugs stopped whining about his head, Mart turned and shouted at Floyd, a dozen feet behind.

"Somebody in that bunch switched sides. Why the hell do you suppose he did that?"

Floyd did not bother to answer. He simply shrugged. The way Floyd rode in his saddle, light and easy on the horse, told Mart what he already knew — that this was not yet finished. Poulos was no fool. He would be fully aware that, if he could kill Mart and Floyd now, the war for Tincup range would be over.

Poulos probably believed that Raoul was dead — had probably been so informed by Howie Frye. Therefore, by his reasoning, if he could not eliminate Mart and Floyd, there would be no one left capable of waging a winning fight for Tincup. Only Lucille Robineau, and it was doubtful if Tincup's crew would fight at all for her. Besides, by the time Lucille found out what was going on, Poulos would be in the middle on Tincup's grass.

Carefully Mart considered the conditions of their horses. They had not exactly spared them this morning, and the animals were bound to be tiring. Mart had no way of knowing how fresh were the mounts of Poulos and his men. Perhaps Poulos had only today ridden up from the desert. If he had, his horses would undoubtedly be worse off than Mart's and Floyd's. On the other hand, if Poulos already had camps established on the plateau, his horses would be reasonably fresh.

They dropped into a gulch, scrambled out, and entered a heavy pocket of aspens — huge, old trees with trunks a foot thick. Mart kept his horse at a steady run now, even though the grade was slightly uphill, for he knew that these first two or three miles were the most important. It would have taken Poulos and his men some time to return to where their horses were tied, to mount, and to give chase. If Mart and his foreman could gain enough of a substantial lead, they would at least be able to set their own pace and not have to worry about bullets singing around their heads.

They broke out of the timber and onto an open trail through the brush. They reached the summit of the grade they were on and plunged deeply into a wide, shallow draw.

Floyd yelled: "We could set an ambush."

But Mart shook his head. Poulos had too many men for that. Down into this draw they went and up its far side. Another just like it lay ahead, perhaps half a mile wide, and they crossed it as well. At the high point on the far side of it, Mart flung a hasty glance over his shoulder. He saw them, a ragged line of galloping riders at the crest of the ridge, the width of the two draws behind them.

A mile? It would not be enough. He projected his mind ahead, recalling the switch-back trail that led off the plateau, that dropped downward into Tincup's valley. A mile lead on that trail would be nothing short of suicide. Poulos could dismount his men at the head of it and pick off Mart and Floyd with rifles, rather like targets in a shooting gallery.

He looked around. Floyd was frowning. Now they angled off to the right slightly, entering a dark pocket of spruce timber. The hoofs of their horses fell almost soundlessly on the thick carpet of needles. A clearing opened up ahead and in it sat a roofless log cabin, a relic of the time when prospectors had roamed this country.

The cabin stirred memories in Mart. He could recall the times, when he was a boy, that he'd brought a blanket and a gunnysack of grub and walked out on top to spend the night at this lonely cabin.

They swept past it and suddenly Mart saw a way out of this. He slowed his horse ever so little, gazing behind at the almost compete lack of tracks behind them on the needle carpet of the little-used trail. He kept slowing the horse and, when he had the animal at a walk, swung off the trail and entered the deep timber, heading straight down towards the rim.

Floyd cursed: "What the hell?"

Mart said: "We'll never ride off the trail without getting killed. Not with the lead we've got. But I used to walk up to that old prospector's cabin when I was a kid. There's a way down through the rim that a man can make afoot. We'll ride as far as the rim, turn the horses loose, and go off afoot. By the time Poulos back-tracks, picks up the place we turned off, and follows us, we'll be clear down in the valley."

Floyd was skeptical. "Depends on who's trackin' for Poulos."

Mart said: "It's the only chance we got."

They had ridden out from the line camp at about one or one-thirty. It was now almost four. Mart was amazed at the swift passage of time. He urged his horse to a trot and faintly heard the drum of hoofs behind him. His ears were attuned to the sound, as he waited for the pause in their rapid cadence, the pause that would tell him his plan had failed, that they had missed his tracks and turned back. But the rapid beat of hoofs did not halt or diminish, and Mart breathed a sigh of relief.

Instantly Floyd's expression lightened. He asked, grinning, "You ever try to draw to an inside straight?"

Mart nodded. "I've done it, too."

"I can believe it . . . after today."

Mart kept angling slightly to the right until he came to the bottom of a steep draw. He followed this for perhaps half a mile and, at last, swung down off his horse. He snatched the rifle from the boot, leaned it against a tree. He flung off saddle and blanket, unbuckled the throat latch on his bridle. He slapped the horse on the rump and sent him trotting up through the timber.

Then he picked up his rifle and slid down off the rim, which at this spot was no more than a dozen feet high. He struck, sliding, still on his feet, and with rapid, running strides went downward across the steep and bushy slope, with Floyd a short ten feet behind him.

By the time Mart reached the ranch house, he was footsore and irritable. He was certainly in no mood simply to sit and wait for Poulos to attack — and attack Mart felt he would surely do. At this hour the place was deserted, save for Fu Ling and Schwartz, the cowpunchers' cook. All of the crew was in the valley above the ranch. The day's branding was undoubtedly finished, and very possibly they were no more than four or five miles away, driving their day's herd before them.

Floyd went at once to the corral, roped out a horse, and saddled.

Mart said: "Make it quick, Floyd. Poulos will be here as soon as he can get off that trail."

Floyd rode out at a dead run, spurring viciously. His temper was aroused, too. Mart figured it would be no more than thirty minutes before Poulos and his riders would arrive. Horseback, they'd have had a much greater distance to travel than had Mart and Floyd. Too, they might have wasted as much as fifteen or twenty minutes trailing their quarry to the rim.

Poulos would be raging, of that Mart was certain. He had

failed to kill them twice today, once when he had them pinned down on the slope above the line camp, and again during the chase when Mart and Floyd had slipped away and crawled off the rim afoot. He would be further enraged by the treachery of one of his own men that had caused his first failure. And in his raging, thwarted mood, Poulos would most certainly attack Tincup as soon as he could get there.

Mart went into the house and gathered up a couple of rifles. He gave one to a scared Fu Ling and stationed the little Chinaman at one of the smaller windows at the front of the house. He had Schwartz take up a vantage point in the barn loft. He himself went into the bunkhouse. And then he waited, his eyes fixed upon the break in the cedars beyond the gate, on the place where Poulos and his men would break off the trail.

The sun sank behind the rim west of the house, and its afterglow stained the thin, horizontal layer of clouds above it a bright, iridescent orange. Then they came, pouring out of the cedars at a brisk trot. They spread as they hit the road and for an instant bunched there, while a thick-set man Mart instantly recognized from Rose's description as Poulos gave his brisk orders. They came in, fanned out across the road in three ranks, twelve or fourteen in all.

Mart raised his rifle, drew a bead on a rider in the front rank. His rifle cracked, and the man pitched to the ground.

As though his shot had been a signal, now a high chorus of yells floated down the valley from Tincup's rapidly approaching 'punchers. Mart began to grin, and then he saw them sweep around a bend. Poulos's men turned to face them. They were not armed for a war, a fact that probably was not at once apparent to Poulos and his men. Yet, what Tincup's 'punchers lacked in guns, they made up for with their yelling. Mart doubted if there were five guns between the whole twenty of them,

188

but those who had guns were firing them as fast as they could shoot.

The ranks of Poulos's riders split, broke backward towards the ranch. Mart howled: "Ling! Schwartz! Pour it on!"

He levered and fired, levered and fired. Two more of Poulos's riders pitched from their saddles.

Poulos stood in his stirrups, waved a thick fist, and bellowed. "Dismount! Take cover!"

Mart ran into the open, beckoned towards the barn, and a moment later Schwartz came running. Mart hung a dozen six-shooters and belts on him, raking them from their nails on the bunkhouse wall. Firing in the lane had slowed to an occasional shot as both sides sought cover and dug in.

Mart said: "Go up the creek for a ways. Circle behind our boys and give them these. With no more guns than they've got, they're licked, only Poulos don't know it yet."

He watched Schwartz disappear into the willows along the creek and then ran across the yard to the house. A bullet plowed a furrow in the ground before him, and he dived into the back door, yelling at once.

"Ling! Come here."

He gathered half a dozen rifles up from various corners of the living room, then tossed several boxes of cartridges into his hat. He handed the weapons and the hat to Ling and repeated the instructions he had given Schwartz. He watched Ling go out the back door, watched him disappear.

Now he ran to the front window of the house, broke the glass with the barrel of his rifle, and poked it through. The yard before him was bare, but the brush began perhaps seventy-five yards from the house — sagebrush, high as a man's shoulders. Poulos's horses milled in the lane, caught between Tincup's fire, Poulos's, and Mart's but, as the firing slacked off, they began to drift into the yard, passed the house, and headed for the creek.

Mart was hoping that Poulos had not noticed how poorly Tincup's bunch had been armed. If he had, if he made a rush before Schwartz and Ling got to them. . . . He shivered. It would be a slaughter.

To try to distract Poulos, he began to fire steadily from the window. He had nothing at which to shoot, nothing but an impenetrable screen of brush, but he fired into it anyway and, after perhaps half a dozen shots, began to draw their answering fire. Bullets slogged into the log walls of the house. One shattered the rest of the window above Mart and showered him with razor-sharp pieces of broken glass.

Light had faded from the sky, from the yard before him. In the gray of dusk an uncertain figure ran across the yard and dived into the barn. Mart fired at him twice, missed both times because of the poor light, and the man's deliberately ragged way of running.

Concern touched him. If Poulos and his hardcases took the buildings, it would be an all night job to dislodge them and an expensive job, expensive in terms of Tincup blood.

Mart dropped the next man that ran across the yard, but he did not kill him. The man crawled until he reached the shelter of the bunkhouse wall.

They came in a rush then, four or five of them. Mart shot twice, and then his rifle clicked emptily. By the time he had yanked out his Colt, the men had reached cover.

From the rear of the house, outside, he heard a hoarse shout. "Get the horses!"

The back door creaked. Swiftly, Mart stooped and pulled off his boots. He ran noiselessly across the huge living room, dropped the stout bar across the front door. He turned. Suddenly he knew how this was to be. Poulos had dropped a man off at the barn, another at the bunkhouse. In a moment Mart knew he would see the glare of fire against the windows of the house, the glare of fires starting in dry hay stored in the barn loft. He knew that the rest of them were in the house.

He tried to remember exactly how many men had run across the yard and felt a little unsure. Six or seven. He'd shot one. He didn't think that one could do much. One in the barn, one in the bunkhouse. That left four probably, maybe five, depending on how badly Mart had hurt the one he shot.

Poulos had known, then, how poorly armed were Tincup's riders. But he had chosen to try and fire the buildings, leaving but three or four men to hold Tincup's crew pinned to the ground so that they could not interfere. Poulos wanted Mart, not the men of Tincup's crew.

The house was almost totally dark now, except for the faint, red glow from the burning barn, a red glow that filtered through the windows and flung its indistinct pattern on the wall. Less than fifteen minutes had elapsed since Mart had sent off Schwartz and Ling.

Keeping his eyes on the kitchen door, Mart twirled the cylinder of the Colt, feeling the blunt-size bullets in the cylinder. He ejected an empty and pushed in a fresh shell. He filled the sixth chamber, the one that was always kept empty for safety's sake. Then he began to advance across the floor, silent and deadly, in his stocking feet.

Suddenly the door flung open, and men spilled into the room. Mart's gun bucked in his hand — twice. Then he raced across the room, dived behind the leather-covered sofa. He had seen a man fall. He knew where that man was hit, knew he would not stir.

Bullets tore through the sofa. A shower of splinters stung Mart's face. He poked his head around, fired at a dim shape against the wall. The man groaned, sagged against the wall,

191

and slid down towards the floor. His gun clattered noisily as it fell.

Two left. Maybe a third in the kitchen. Mart was positive of his count this time. Four men had come through the door, and none of them had been Poulos.

He ejected the three empties, poked fresh shells into the gun's loading gate. He eased back the hammer and spoke into the darkness.

"Who's next, boys?"

He did not know Corbin, but it was Corbin who spoke. "Would you let a man ride out? This is a damned fool play. If we kill you, they'll hunt us down."

Mart asked: "Poulos in the kitchen?"

"Uh-huh."

"Who's with him?"

"He's alone."

Mart laughed softly. "Don't blame you for wanting out. All right. Toss your guns against the wall, one at a time, so I can count them."

"Man, we can't get out of here without guns."

"Then you don't get out."

The man sighed. "All right."

A gun thumped against the wall. Another. Mart knew that Poulos, in the kitchen, had heard all this. He tried to figure when the man would make his play. Not now. He had been betrayed by these two. He would not trust them again. He would figure them as being against him.

Mart was down behind the sofa. He was covered. He knew he ought to wait there. Tincup 'punchers would be spilling into the kitchen door any minute now.

Corbin muttered, "How do we get out of here?"

"Walk past me, one at a time. Your hands over your head. Be careful, boys. I'm pretty nervous."

A man's shape loomed at the end of the sofa, another right behind him. Mart lifted his gun. He knew suddenly when Poulos would strike. He knew it would be when these men drew abreast of him, when his attention was distracted. Suddenly it occurred to Mart that he had let himself fall into as nice a trap as had ever been devised. He knew he could thank Howie for it. He could almost hear Howie's words as he said, *"Mart's got a soft streak in him."*

Poulos had counted on that soft streak. Now it was going to cost Mart his life.

Chapter Twenty

He was raging. Fury, greater than any he had ever known before, pounded through his body, raised its smoky fumes to his brain. He knew there was only one thing to do. He knew what it was, and he raised his gun. But he could not do it, and instantly realized why he could not. It was not in him to guess when human life was at stake.

He had made a bargain with these two, had agreed to let them leave. He was now sure they did not intend to leave, instead would jump him as Poulos came through the kitchen door. They had rid themselves of two guns, but they were not unarmed. Each would have a holdout gun. They would break their part of the bargain but, until they did, Mart was chained to his.

All this in the racing fraction of a second. Mart's muscles tensed. Raw fury turned him reckless, made him swift and sure. He bounded to his feet, eyes on the kitchen door, not on the two approaching him. They would be slowed by surprise. Their hands were over their heads.

He saw at once that he had been right. Poulos was there in the doorway, faintly lighted by the red glow of the fire that filtered through the windows. Poulos, squat and sure, gun in hand.

Poulos's gun centered itself on Mart, followed his movements unwaveringly. Mart flung himself against the wall with a resounding crash and then, with the steadiness of the wall against him, centered his gun on Poulos and tightened his finger on the trigger. He was steady enough to shoot. He was also for an instant still enough for Poulos to shoot at him. The roar of Poulos's gun was ear-shattering in the enclosed room.

Mart had the racing, exultant thought, *Missed!* The hammer fell on his own gun and flame laced from its muzzle. The feel of the gun as it fired told him instantly that he was all right. He shoved his shoulder against the wall and came violently away from it, falling and not trying to stop. The two stood across the room, beyond the long sofa. One of them held a long-barreled Colt, the other a small and deadly Derringer. Its noise was a crack compared to the roar of the Colt, but just as deadly. Two bullets thudded into the wall behind where Mart had been.

His own gun bucked again in his hand, and the bullet tore a leg out from under the gunman who held the Colt. Mart was rolling by then, off balance, and could not bring his gun to bear. He saw the gaping muzzle of the Derringer, saw it steady on his prone body. Mart knew at once that he would never stop that shot, that this was the one which no one could stop.

Then a gun crashed in the kitchen doorway. Confusion stirred in Mart. He would have sworn he had killed Poulos. His gun had felt so right when it fired.

Not until he saw the gunman driven back by the force of a bullet did the realization come to him that it was a rifle, not a revolver, which had fired from the door.

Floyd's hoarse voice, frantic, came bellowing into the room. "Mart! Mart, you hurt?"

Mart scrambled to his feet, still edgy enough to cover the crippled gunman. His voice sounded hoarse and cracked, not his own.

"No. But I sure as hell would have been in a minute."

Tincup 'punchers crowded in around him. A couple of them yanked the wounded gunman to his feet and hustled him out into the kitchen. Others began at once the task of dragging bodies from the room. A man stooped and began to gather up bits of broken glass from a shattered lamp.

Floyd's words rushed out like a flood. "Mart, we couldn't do a damned thing. The boys kind of quit packing guns during calf branding. There was only four guns amongst us. We were pinned down, and we damned well knew it. Schwartz got there first, and Ling was right behind him. We moved right along after that."

Mart fished in his pocket and found a match. He raised the glass chimney of a lamp and touched the flame to the wick.

He asked: "Poulos dead?"

"Uh-huh. Dead center."

Floyd was staring at him, concern and a certain doubt in his expression. Mart could almost read his thoughts. He was wondering what this would do to Mart. He was thinking what the slaughter of a bunch of sheep had done to him. . . .

Reaction set in with Mart. He shivered violently. He tossed his gun at the sofa and walked to the front door. He raised the heavy bar and went out on the porch.

Cold air was good in his nostrils, against his heated, sweating face. But he could not stop his shivering. He sat down on the step and dropped his face into his hands. He heard Floyd come onto the porch behind him. Floyd sat down beside him, not touching him, not speaking for a long while.

Finally Floyd said: "They tried to burn Tincup. They tried to kill you, and they tried to kill me. It's like shooting wolves, Mart."

Mart looked at the blazing barn, at the bunkhouse fire now coming under control from the bucket line that stretched to the pump. At last he stood up. He was steady now, not shaking any more. He looked at Floyd and shrugged. A hint of his old grin spread across his face.

He had thought it out, there on the steps. There were times when a man had no choice. He killed, or he was killed himself. It was a satisfaction to him now that he had played this out his own way to the very end. It would help him in the months to come. He could have downed those two gunmen from the comparative safety of concealment behind the old sofa and then turned to Poulos. But he had not. He had given his word, and only their treachery had broken it.

Wearily he stumped down the steps and went across the yard. It would be morning before Tincup was entirely safe. But in work, in hard, physical work, was to be found release from the intolerable tension of the last hour.

Near midnight one of the guards who had been with Raoul galloped into the yard and halted his horse to gaze with awe-stricken eyes at the wreckage, at the line of bodies laid out evenly before the porch. Subdued, he sought out Mart.

"Your wife's dead, Boss. She fell from a ledge outside Raoul's window whilst she was trying to kill him. Raoul's all right. So's Rose."

What were the things Mart felt? Regret? Pity? Yes, both of these. Yet he only nodded shortly in thanks and then went back to work. When finally the last ember was extinguished, when the last of the wounded had been loaded into wagons for the trip to Cedar City, he stumped wearily into the house. Then, and only then, was he about to sleep.

Howie Frye was dead. A detachment of heavily armed Tincup riders had found his body on the slope above the old line camp where he had fallen. His corpse now lay inside a new pine coffin on Tincup's long verandah.

Sheep, a steady, bleating stream, moved rapidly towards the trail that would take them off Tincup grass. Their herders, subdued, kept glancing back over their shoulders as though completely terrified. And a long line of pack horses, each bearing a grim reminder for the future to the desert sheepmen, filed down off the steep trail and onto the broad, flat reaches of desert.

Joe Herdic's jail was jammed with survivors. Doc Saunders was busy among the wounded.

Mart Joliffe had not left Tincup. Somehow he felt that all of the bad things had left it untouched. If good things were to come in the future, they must begin here.

Out of Cedar City rolled the yellow-wheeled buckboard, crowded, bearing three on its narrow seat.

Raoul Joliffe sat at the reins, gaunt and fierce, an odd glow lighting in his eyes. He popped the whip savagely to urge the hot-blooded bay team to even greater speed.

Cris Lesback, Cedar City's part-time preacher, sat beside him, white-faced, nervously exhorting Raoul to slow down.

But Tincup lay ahead. Tincup lay ahead, and Raoul only laughed.

Rose Frye, the third person on the buckboard seat, smiled. In her eyes was the wild, fierce joy of a woman coming home to her man.

About the Author

Lewis B. Patten wrote more than ninety Western novels in thirty years, and three of them won Golden Spur Awards from the Western Writers of America, and the author received the Golden Saddleman Award. Indeed, this points up the most remarkable aspect of his work: not that there is so much of it, but that so much of it is so fine. Patten was born in Denver, Colorado, and served in the U. S. Navy 1933–1937. He was educated at the University of Denver during the war years and became an auditor for the Colorado Department of Revenue during the 1940s. It was in this period that he began contributing significantly to Western pulp magazines, fiction that was from the beginning fresh and unique and revealed Patten's lifelong concern with the sociological and psychological affects of group psychology on the frontier. He became a professional writer at the time of his first novel, *Massacre at White River* (1952). The dominant theme in much of his fiction is the notion of justice, and its opposite, injustice. In his first novel it has to do with exploitation of the Ute Indians, but as he matured as a writer he explored this theme with significant and poignant detail in small towns throughout the early West. Crimes, such as rape or lynching, are often at the center of his stories. When the values embodied in these small towns are examined closely, they are found to be wanting. Conformity is always easier than taking a stand. Yet, in Patten's view of the American West, there is usually a man or a woman who refuses to conform. Among his finest titles, always a difficult choice, surely are *A Killing at Kiowa* (1972), *Ride a Crooked Trail* (1976), and his

199

many fine contributions to Doubleday's Double D series, including *Villa's Rifles* (1977), *The Law at Cottonwood* (1978), and *Death Rides a Black Horse* (1978). *The Trail to Vicksburg* is the second of his hitherto unpublished novels that will next appear as a **Five Star Western.**

3/97   4   1/97

2/98   4.   1/97